# Naomi's Journey Into The Light

## A Novel

*All my best,*
*—Sam Rawlins*

## Sam Rawlins

TULSA

*Naomi's Journey Into The Light*
ISBN: 978-1-957262-16-1 (Paperback)
        978-1-957262-25-3 (Ebook)

Copyright TX 9-080-538 © 2022 by Sam Rawlins

Printed in the USA. First edition 2022

Yorkshire Publishing
1425 E 41st Pl
Tulsa, OK 74105
www.YorkshirePublishing.com
918.394.2665

# Dedication

For Margie, Fernie, and June:
My life has been truly blessed with
your friendship and support.
It has meant the world to me.

# CONTENTS

## CHAPTER 1

# A Look Back

Have you ever had a personal encounter with God? I have pondered that question many times in my life.

Someone once told me that a person who has actually made contact with the Lord knows more about God than one who has just read about Him. Before I explain further, I must first go back to a time a little over ten years ago. So that you might better understand my story, a short narrative of what happened during those years will be helpful. The memories take shape within my mind as still painful images when I think about it.

My name is Naomi Larson. I had just turned eighteen and was in my last week of high school. Everything was upbeat and positive in my life. But then I learned my mother was fatally ill. Her prognosis was dim. The doctors said she had only weeks to live. My life changed overnight.

My father and I were both devastated. Mom had been our whole world. She had been our rock, the one who had inspired faith in both of us.

I went to visit her in the hospital during her last few days. I said, "Hello Mom," in the most cheerful voice I could summon up.

"My girl," she responded, an immediate appearance of warmth filling her face. "Please come in, pull up a chair. I've been thinking about something I want to talk to you about." She motioned to a chair near her hospital bed.

I did as she asked, pulling up a chair beside her. Reaching over, I took her hand into mine. It was quite cold to the touch. Circulation was already leaving her body. I felt a sense of urgency, asking her, "What is it, Mom? What did you want to tell me?"

She explained slowly, still thinking about it, "Things happen in our lives that we have no control over, things that leave us asking questions. When I was a young girl, I went sledding in winter. The pond was frozen over, but the ice was thin. Climbing up on the bank, I lost my footing and fell backward. I would've fallen through the ice and might have froze to death. As I was going backward, it was as if an invisible hand pushed me back up on the bank. To this day, I feel like my life was saved by an unseen angel. I guess the moral of my story is since that incident, I started believing God is involved in our lives more than we think. It's something I want you to remember, Naomi."

"You mean as sick as you are, God is somehow involved?"

"Yes, I believe, even now, God is somehow involved. He has a reason for everything."

"Mom, you're a good person."

"I believe the Lord knows best in all things. We are all His children. There are those that seem to forget that."

I squeezed her hand tenderly, with all the love I felt for her. I would always remember her saying, *we are all God's children.*

Later that evening, something inside me urged me to go back to the hospital. Upon seeing her, I could tell she was nearing the end. As tears formed in my eyes, she looked up at me and whispered, "Honey, don't cry for me. I'm going home to God."

I had gone back to comfort her. Instead, she had comforted me. My mother was a very great lady, a devout person of faith. The words within the Bible were sacred to her.

Sitting next to my mother on her last day alive, I could clearly see she could barely breathe. She was drowning in her own body fluids which were rapidly filling her lungs. It was agonizing and heartbreaking to see. She was suffocating, and I knew it. When she died, I think a part of me also died.

After she was gone, my father took me home and left me alone in my bedroom. I sat on the floor, shaking and crying uncontrollably. I had always thought she would be there. My heart was broken.

As I sat there, I became rapidly filled with regret for all

the things I had not said to her or things I had not done with her. Reaching over, I picked up a nearby framed picture of my mother holding me as a baby. Studying the loving expression on her face, I whispered, "Please, Mom, I will never stop loving you. You had a kind, compassionate heart. Yet, you were strong and full of courage when you needed to be. If only I could be just as strong right now...."

I wept again, consumed by grief that tore into the deepest parts of my soul. Through my eighteen years of young life, I had no real understanding of death. The reality of her passing hit me like a ton of bricks.

I was emotionally broken by my mother's death. There is no quick fix for such grief. I needed an understanding shoulder to lean on. The one person who could've helped me heal—my father—turned away from me.

One morning I looked across the dining table and saw the man my father had turned into. He had become a stranger who I no longer recognized. His capacity for love and understanding was gone. He blamed me for everything wrong in our home after Mom died. His grief twisted into bitterness as he blurted out, "Your mother was such a class act. You'll never measure up to her! I don't even like to think about you. You're such a failure!"

We had come to an emotional crossroads. His verbal abuse became constant, escalating to the point where I could no longer take it. He lashed out at me with an expression of hate on his face that I can't erase from my memory, "In some way, you must be responsible for her death. Yes, you're the reason she died!"

I think it was at that moment I decided I could no longer live under the same roof with this man. It felt like I was being emotionally ripped apart. Our bond as father and daughter was broken. If I stayed, I knew I was going to have a mental breakdown. I had to do something, so I decided to leave. Three days later I went down to the bus station, bought a ticket and left home for good.

Even though I left, I soon found out I could not escape my father's words. They stayed with me, haunting me, leaving me with crushing low self-esteem. I felt less than worthless for a long time after leaving home. Every time I looked in a mirror, all I saw was a loser. I drifted aimlessly from one state to another.

Over the next ten years, I traveled from small-town middle America to the west coast. During the entire time, I couldn't shake the feeling I was drowning–drowning in a sea of depression. My life had no purpose. I was just surviving, from one odd job to another.

It's difficult to explain. It felt like I was living in a kind of darkness. There was no light in my life. I was just existing, not actually living. I knew I needed help. I was lost, adrift in the sea of life without a compass.

One day while I was walking the streets of a city along the west coast, someone pressed a small pocket Bible into my hands. The young man, who was a stranger to me, said this,

"Read this, you look like you need it." Before I could say anything, he quickly left.

As I glanced down at the little Bible in my hands, it made me think about the faith that was no longer in my mind and heart. When my mother died, the faith she so strongly embraced left me. Actually, though, the truth was I sort of left it.

I thought about my present lack of faith as I stood frozen on a busy downtown sidewalk. For a moment, I focused on the memory of my mother reading the Bible to me when I was a child. Just the thought made me hunger for the words in it. Taking the pocket Bible back to my hotel room, I started reading it, especially pouring over chapters about the life and crucifixion of Jesus. I found myself turning to God for answers. Reading it, over and over, Christ's words somehow opened a tiny window in my mind, letting in a ray of hope.

I originally thought the young man handing me the pocket Bible on the street was a random act of fate. Now I'm not so sure. I've come to believe that God takes an active part in influencing the events of our lives more often than we realize.

For years I had not been feeling quite right within myself. The chains of my past were still wrapped tightly around me. I kept suppressing those feelings, pushing them deeper and deeper within myself. But finally, sort of an epiphany came to me. Within the deepest inner sanctum of the human mind lies a small hidden chamber containing our most troubling thoughts. I resolved to examine those thoughts one night. I was just beginning to do so when I fell into a deep sleep.

A dream as real as life itself quickly seized me. Without realizing it, I had been nearing the point of both mental and physical exhaustion. So it was, the most life-like image of my mother came into the room, sitting down beside my bed. Seeing her convinced me that people who have been close to us in life talk to us after they've passed on.

I looked up into her eyes, which penetrated me as she spoke, "I'm here because you need to get your life back on track. You must return to your roots. There you will find yourself and be reborn in the light."

"Mom, you're here," I said, still not quite believing I was seeing and hearing her. "You look so well now," I said, seeing that she was completely healed from her illness.

Her voice seemed to speak to my soul as she whispered, "I'm okay now. I'm with God."

"Oh, Mom!" my voice was full of awe and wonder as I reached out to touch her. But as I did so, she vanished completely. I woke up immediately, both startled and quite moved by what had just happened.

Sitting up on the side of the bed, I thought about this dream. But was it just a dream? Does the Lord sometimes come to us when we are asleep and plant thoughts of things He wants us to do? What had been weighing heavily on my mind had come to me in this way.

My mother *was* here. She *was* completely real. Trying to make sense of it, I wondered, does the soul separate from the physical body when one dies? Did the Lord allow some part of her soul to counsel me from the hereafter, especially when I needed her the most? As I tried to get back to sleep, the questions lingered with me.

The dream was so vivid. It kept replaying in my head throughout the next morning. I kept hearing my mother's voice: *You need to return to your hometown. There you will be reborn in the light.* What did this mean? Should I, could I make this dream a reality?

Later, I went to lunch downtown. I was sitting in a restaurant where I could hear people at a nearby table behind me. One spoke up to a friend, "You should really go back home. Re-connect with that small town. It might do you some good."

It was as if the man were talking to me. His advice resonated with what I'd been thinking inside my head. I found myself asking, what did I want to do with the rest of my life? All morning I'd been coming to the conclusion that I'd been just existing, living in a negative bubble for several years. I resolved to replace it, striving for a better, more positive life.

I guess the events of the last 24 hours were meant to be, for I listened to what all the voices were telling me to do. I went down to the bus station and bought a ticket that would take me back to my hometown. It would take me into an unexpected future, into something I knew nothing about.

From my dream, my mother's words would become a reality.

# CHAPTER 2

# Return To Holdenville

During the long bus trip from the west coast, many thoughts ran through my head. I thought about my suffering. At one time or another, I think we all have suffered pain in our lives. My own mental anguish was lingering inside me. I was hoping that coming back to my hometown would somehow be part of the healing process for me.

Before I left the coast, I saw a sort of emptiness in many people. A sort of directionless life seemed to have taken root in so many lives. To live without hope is a horrible way to live. I know that now. It has become clear to me that there has been a growing hunger for the Lord's presence in the lives of all humankind.

On the bus, I resolved I would start becoming a better person. This would be a work in progress, something I would be willing to dedicate the rest of my life to doing.

After being visited by my mother's spirit, I had become convinced that there was something bigger than me, bigger than all of us, urging me forward. Whatever it was, I knew I needed to find it. I was becoming a believer that all of this was coming from a higher power.

The object of my goal was getting closer. Holdenville is just a little way off the interstate. If you blink, you might miss the turnoff. It's a small town of little more than a thousand people.

Arriving at the bus station on the west side of town, I felt both happy and sad to be back. I was happy to see long-cherished places from my childhood once again. On the other hand, I had already decided not to see my father. I was sad about returning alone and forgotten, uneasy about facing an uncertain future.

A strange feeling ran through me. As I stepped off the bus, it felt like the ground shook beneath my feet. A blast of frigid air cut right through my coat. At the same time, it felt like a sharp cold knife. I was immediately reminded it was February and still winter in Holdenville. A terrible ice storm had hit just days before I arrived.

After getting off the bus, I stood motionless for a moment. Staring up at the sky, it was dull and overcast, all metallic gray in color, covering the entire town in a blanket of depression.

Stepping forward, I went into this cold, bleak atmosphere. Reacting to the wind, I pulled my coat tighter around myself and set out eastward across downtown.

At first glance, looking down Main Street, my reaction was that the sands of time move very slowly. All of the buildings were the same structures that dated back to the 1940s and early 1950s.

I walked up to a mirror in the window of the old drug store that had stood there for more than seventy-five years. I hadn't stared in that window since I graduated from high school. Back then, the young girl's reflection was full of innocence. The image I saw now reflected a world-weary face, tired and worn down. The shadows of a troubled world had erased any appearance of my youth.

Walking a short distance, I took the first turn off Main Street, hoping a change of scenery would stop the unwanted recall. Walking over to Second Street, the atmosphere there was quieter, with far less activity. It was a narrow street with only one lane of traffic running each way. No new buildings were on this street either. Mostly old residential structures were here.

Up ahead, though, toward the end of this block, stood an old three-story building. Standing out in an otherwise residential neighborhood, it was built during Holdenville's faded glory days. Even though I wasn't looking for it, I felt drawn toward this particular structure for some unknown reason. Perhaps, it was the large sign above its front door that caught my eye. What was this place? Getting closer, I could make out what the sign read: ALL SOULS HOSPICE.

It was then I remembered hearing my mother talk about this place almost 20 years ago. She had seen an article on the front page of the *Holdenville Daily World* newspaper. This was the old building that had been turned into a place for severely ill people in their last weeks or months of life.

Staring up at the sign, there was something hypnotic about it. I was being drawn toward the door. Should I go inside? The need to find a place to pray took hold of me all of a sudden. I wondered, might there be a chapel inside?

Trying to decide if I should act upon my impulse, in the quiet of the moment, a God-like voice inside my head whispered to me, *Come in here, for your burden is great. Come unto me, and I will give you peace.* It was the most magnetic, commanding voice I'd ever heard. I knew I must listen to it. Hesitating no longer, I opened the door and entered. I've never been the same since.

At the time, I wondered about the voice that spoke to my mind. I had never heard it before. Whose voice was it? I did not have to wonder for long, for I would be in the presence of its owner soon....It was the voice of Christ.

## CHAPTER 3

# Chaplain Andrews

When I was standing outside, I had thought that many people go through their entire lives trying to justify their reasons for living. An inner need to validate my own existence was pulling me inside to pray.

As I think about it now, I didn't just walk through the doors of *All Souls Hospice* by myself. God was with me. His will was inside me, urging me forward.

Entering this building would become the single most important thing I had ever done. Something good and righteous had reached deep within my soul and drew me inside.

Glancing around the lobby, I noticed the lighting in the room projected a golden warmth that was in stark contrast to the cold and gray look of the outside world. Immediately, I picked up on a hard-to-define energy that seemed to flow like a gentle breeze throughout the room. It set me at peace with the strangest of feelings. All at once, I felt like I belonged here.

Just then, I looked up to see a man of about forty emerging from a hallway across the lobby. Carrying a Bible, he made immediate eye contact with me. His attitude seemed friendly even before he uttered a word. Right away, he projected an understanding aura as he spoke to me in a soft-spoken voice, introducing himself, "I'm Chaplain Andrews. May I help you?"

I explained, "I was looking for a place to pray. Might you have such a place?"

He was welcoming, "If you want to pray, our chapel is the soul of this hospice. It's truly a place where you can seek God. As the Bible says, He is our refuge and strength, a very present help in time of trouble."

I took his words to heart and confessed, "I certainly need His help now."

Seeing an expression of need on my face, he reached out to me, "If you'd like to talk later, I want you to know I'm here."

"It's been a long time since I've had anyone care about me or my feelings. But if you don't mind, though, I do have a question or two."

"Yes, by all means, ask me anything you'd like."

"When I first came through your doors, I sensed something strange, like a breeze, but again it wasn't."

"I know exactly what you're talking about. Over time, I

have come to understand it clearly. A form of spiritual energy has been found to be circulating throughout the entire building for years. Without question, it comes straight from God."

At that moment, I was caught up in the sincerity of his explanation, replying simply, "I believe you."

Just then, I think he saw something in me he liked, telling me, "I think, in your heart, you're a person of faith as well. Thank you for believing me. While you're here, I hope you will see, as I see, that this building is a sacred place, blessed by the Lord."

"Do you think others may feel this way, and that's why they come in here to pray?"

"Perhaps some believe this, but I think most come in here to pray for much more personal reasons. They feel like our chapel is a place where they can truly open up to God."

As I looked up into his face, it was as though I could see much deeper than 'skin deep.' I told him what my eyes saw, "Chaplain Andrews, you have a beautiful soul."

Reacting, his eyes searched my face for a moment. It was as if he saw something no one else could see or know, including myself. Then he responded, without revealing the truth of what he was saying to me, "God works in mysterious ways."

I was curious, not really understanding what he was trying to convey. I asked him, explaining, "I don't understand. What are you trying to say?"

Strangely, he avoided answering me then. "I will explain

when you're finished in our chapel. Then–please–come by and see me in my office. We will talk, and you will understand my words then."

I still wondered, but I let it go, already feeling a growing trust in Chaplain Andrews. Reassuring him, I said, "I'll visit with you when I'm finished in your chapel, I promise."

I made this commitment, not completely realizing how sacred a promise was here. I would keep it, though because I was already beginning to feel the strong presence of God within these walls.

The two of us continued to stare at each other for a brief moment. It was as though we both had just met someone who would linger on in importance to each other.

Interrupting the silence, he wanted to know more about me, "You know, I don't know your name."

"Oh, I'm sorry, I'm Naomi Larson."

He responded, "I'm Stephen Andrews, Chaplain here. Ms. Naomi, if I may ask, why did you come in here to pray?"

"It just happened, like fate. When I got off the bus this morning, I thought I was going to conduct all my business over on Main Street. I was walking along when I got a sudden impulse to walk over to Second Street, where time seemed to slow down. I glanced around, taking in all the old structures here. It was almost an accident that I even saw this building. But when I did, I had a sudden urge to check and see if you had a facility where I might pray."

I could see the wheels of thought turning within

Chaplain Andrews as he spoke, "I prefer to think it was more destiny than anything else that brought you here."

"Why do you say that?"

"Fate often implies some sort of accident that it even happened. On the other hand, destiny implies something greater than all of us brought you here."

"I must admit," I conceded, "it felt like some invisible force was pushing me this way."

"For whatever the reason, fate or destiny, I believe it's a good thing you found your way to *All Souls.*"

"Maybe God will answer my prayers in your chapel. Maybe He will look into my troubled heart and make all things come together for good."

We walked across the lobby, going past an elevator and staircase that led to the upper floors and on to the entrance into the hallway. It was wider so that wheelchairs could easily navigate its length to the chapel entrance at the far end of the hall.

Immediately inside the hall, to my right, was the chaplain's office and his quarters. Glancing ahead of us, this pathway to the chapel was vacant with the exception of several lights anchored on wall sconces on both sides of the hall.

As we proceeded down the hallway, it felt like a meaningful friendship with Chaplain Andrews was beginning. So, I asked him about his faith, "Stephen, how is it you became a chaplain?"

Turning to me, he spoke about his own encounter with

the Lord, "I heard a voice. God saw something in me that I'd never seen in myself. It was a moment that simple. It led me into a lifetime commitment that has turned out to be much greater than myself."

I opened up a little more, "This morning, I had no thought I would wind up in a hospice today. Sometimes it seems life has been full of surprises for me."

"Some say it's also full of miracles. Perhaps what your heart has been wanting is a miracle."

"A miracle? You mean the kind that might be life-changing?"

Somehow Chaplain Andrews' insight into my feelings was incredibly correct, "A miracle might be exactly what you need, Naomi. You will never be able to escape your soul's deep need. Think on it."

The way he said it struck home to me. In my heart, I knew he was right.

Taking a few steps further, he gestured to the double doors just ahead of us and said, "Beyond those doors is the living, beating heart of *All Souls Hospice*."

I was sincerely grateful, "Thank you for showing me the way."

He added, "May God show you the rest of the way."

Turning my attention back toward the chapel doors, it felt like something more powerful than anything on Earth was just beyond them.

# CHAPTER 4

# A Vision

Entering the chapel, I knew immediately that I was in a sacred place. I knew this because I was where I might seek the Lord.

No one appeared to be here. The complete silence in this place of worship was profound in the sense that I felt a presence here. I would soon find it to be the presence of God.

Here, I felt protected from all the turmoil outside the walls of this building. Millions of people go through life feeling lost. For right now, in this moment of time, I was no longer one of them. I felt safe, yet a sensation like I'd never experienced was closing in on me.

As I stood motionless just inside the chapel, a strange tingling seemed to run from my feet, coursing upward through my entire body. A feeling of being surrounded by something all-powerful seized me. For whatever reason, God's hand was involved.

Call it a premonition, but even then, it seemed like another realm of existence was about to open up before me. I had the strongest feeling I was going to find a path that could change the course of my life forever.

Just then, an unknown source of light came out of nowhere and lit up the whole chapel. My eyes traveled up a shaft of light that had penetrated through one of the large cathedral windows along the wall.

Focusing on the sky outside, revealed a series of clouds moving in. The ray of illuminating sunshine would be blocked out. I could almost feel the calm before an impending storm. The sounds of wind picking up, they were blowing through trees just outside, bending limbs against the building. Perhaps a storm was coming soon, or was it more that something was happening just inside my mind?

From the back, my view took in the whole chapel. It was a small auditorium, consisting of perhaps ten rows of seats leading to an altar table facing them. A large, gleaming metallic cross was anchored to the center of the table.

While the rows of seating fell into dark shadows, the altar was well lit by unseen ceiling lights just above and behind it. This lighting was warm and golden, welcoming me.

I felt something powerfully spiritual as my eyes focused upon the cross. Something about it reached inside my mind and spoke to my soul. I recognized it as the same voice that spoke to my mind when I first entered through the doors of *All Souls Hospice.*

I remembered what my mother had taught me: The Kingdom of God is within you and all who believe. Yet even though I knew better, fear of the unknown still lingered inside me.

That's when I heard His voice, *Naomi, let go of your fears. Come unto me, for I will make all things come together for good in you.*

"Yes, Lord," I answered, now knowing it was God speaking to my mind. "I will come."

The Voice that spoke to my inner self invited me to approach His altar. I knew the spirit of God, which transcends all human understanding, would be there. I wondered, had I found God, or did He find me? It didn't really matter, though, for something was happening that would change my life for all time.

I started walking down the center aisle that cut through the middle of the auditorium to the altar down in front. Passing rows of seating on either side of me, I focused on the luminescent cross ahead of me. The energy emanating from it was drawing me. A glowing light around it seemed to expand, looming larger as I got closer. Increasingly, this cross represented everything that was holy to me.

With each succeeding step, all the heartbreaks of my life came rushing back to me. All the hurt and pain within me rose to the surface. Regret for things I had said or left unsaid filled me.

As I reached the altar, all the anguish stored up over a lifetime was boiling over within me. I wanted to pray, laying the heavy weight of all my burdens before God.

Standing right in front of the altar table, I stared directly into the intense light surrounding the cross. Reaching out, I touched its smooth metal surface. Running my fingers across it, I thought about the pain and suffering of Jesus Christ. After that, an almost endless stream of emotions and feelings ran through my mind.

Somehow, I had awakened a powerful force from within this cross. Something invisible was closing in all around me. Though unseen, I knew it was a very spiritual presence.

Awed by what was happening, I took a step backward from the altar table. Bowing my head in sincere respect to my Lord and my God, I knew I needed His help. Clasping my hands, I poured out my feelings in prayer, "Oh Lord, please help me. Show me the way. Come back into my life."

Reaching out for support, I braced myself against the altar table. Opening up my whole heart and soul to my Savior, I added, "In Jesus' holy name, I pray. Please forgive me for leaving you, for losing my faith. I know now you were always there. I have felt so worthless these past ten years without you in my life. I come as a lost sheep back into the fold. Please change me, within and without, to be a better person. I'll do anything for you, Lord, anything."

Sensing it in the chapel, I knew He was searching my

heart and knew my prayer was sincere and real. Feeling His healing warmth penetrate me, it was as though a great weight had been lifted from me.

Grateful, my eyes became focused on the cross again. Through this symbol of Christ's crucifixion, I had sought God in a way that was far deeper than just words in a prayer. With all my heart and soul, I had wanted to feel His presence surrounding me, cleansing and redeeming me.

But much more than I ever thought possible was happening. Right in front of me, the light emanating from within the cross became brighter, more intense than ever. It expanded into an aura, enveloping me.

A power far greater than mortal man was making this happen, transporting my life essence to another time and place. The chapel and its surroundings vanished completely, leaving me to only guess what was happening. The brilliant light also vanished, only to reveal a world of harsh landscapes being consumed by the cruelest of time.

I found myself struggling to get up a steep, rocky hill. I didn't know why. I just knew I had to get to the top. Slipping to my hands and knees, I crawled over sharp, cutting rocks.

Being far removed from the chapel, I asked myself, where was I? Was I dreaming? It was far too vivid, too real to be so. Could this be some sort of vision?

Rather through self-induced hypnosis or something more profoundly God-induced, I had to be in this place for a reason.

Pushing forward up the ridge in front of me, I reached something of a plateau. Just as I got to where it levels off, a mob swarmed past me. Many were shouting, yelling, and clashing with one another.

In a sense, I had become one with the times I had traveled into. By that, I mean I was dressed as people from that time period. I had the appearance of belonging here, yet I knew I was from another place across time.

It was a scorching day. There was dust and heat everywhere.

Rushing forward from behind me, another mass of angry people pushed me to the ground. The atmosphere was filled with hate all around me. Many foamed at the mouth as they spewed out mean-spirited anger. Satan himself had taken possession of these people.

Still on my knees, my view–though greatly obscured by the mass of people in front of me–was a gently rising craggy incline that rose into a more leveled area up ahead. The ground was desolate, devoid of any moisture. A foreboding feeling came over me that this was a place where horrible things happened.

Just then, a hand thrust into view right in front of my face. My eyes followed up to its owner. I found myself staring into the face of the most compassionate-looking young man I'd ever seen. "Here, take my hand," he said.

With his assistance, I rose to my feet again. Now I could see the crowd seemed to be gathering around something going on along the horizon, just up ahead. I asked the young man, "What is this place?"

"Some call it the place of the skull because it resembles that from a distance. But its name is Golgotha Hill. It's where the Romans carry out their executions."

As we made our way forward, the young man continued, "It's a horrible time to be alive." As he said those words, the expression on his face told me his heart was breaking.

I didn't want to believe what was happening. Having that awful sense of foreboding rising up inside me again, I still had to ask, "Who are they executing today?"

"By order of Governor Pilate, they are crucifying my Lord and Master. He once told me this would happen."

"What exactly did He tell you?"

"He told me that He was going to have to die to pay for the sins of all mankind."

As the young man walked on ahead of me, the crowd seemed to part right in front of him. I froze, getting a clear view of three crosses along the horizon.

It was then I knew. I was present at the crucifixion of Christ. How was this possible? I wondered if I had been caught up in some kind of fevered dream. Yet, the look of everything seemed so authentic and genuine. Even the smell was real. This was more than a vision. I WAS THERE! For some reason yet to be known to me, I was witnessing one of the darkest days in all history, two thousand years ago.

Christ's crucifixion was actually happening right in

front of me in real-time. Realizing this, I cannot begin to tell you what I was feeling at that moment, but I'm sure all my emotions were off the charts.

Advancing through the crowd toward the cross, I could see the figure of Christ nailed to it. In their furious hatred of Him, Jesus had been tortured to almost the point of death. His whole body reflected the anguish He was in.

As I got closer, I could clearly see His face. The deep furrows burrowed deep across His forehead. Streams of blood flowed down from the crown of thorns crushed into it. His eyes, meeting mine, connected us. I was transfixed. I felt His unconditional love penetrating my heart. I started crying. It tore at my soul, seeing what was happening.

His expression was hypnotic, reaching deep inside me. He seemed to be staring right into my mind. He was so full of compassion for me. I felt His love for all of humanity in that brief incredible moment. It was part of the miracle of Jesus.

For the first time in my life, I think I was beginning to understand who Christ was and the true meaning of His sacrifice. He was greater than any man who had ever lived.

There were those who had gathered nearby, yelling and cursing at Him. I knew in my heart that He was being crucified by the wickedness of these men. They could not understand He was dying to atone for their sins and all our sins.

In response to those men and all evil doers, His words were full of compassion and love, "Father, forgive them, for they know not what they do."

As I looked up at Him, I heard His human voice for the first time. The sound of that voice in agony has haunted me ever since. It has stayed with me and will probably do so all the rest of my life. The power of those words not only penetrated deep into my heart that day but spread across two thousand years of time into the hearts and minds of all humanity.

Standing near the foot of the cross now, I gazed back up at Jesus. His contorted body pushed upward on the nails impaling Him. Sinking to my knees, I avoided the sight of His tearing flesh. Not able to absorb the impact of what I'd seen, my whole body shook with emotion. For one brief moment, I felt as if I was being crucified myself. My heart was breaking for Him. A spontaneous plea broke from my lips, "Oh God, please help Him!"

"My child," the voice of Jesus broke the silence. The sound of His voice went straight through me. I looked back up into His battered face as our eyes met again. He was able to see my inner turmoil and whispered, "It was for this I was born to atone for the sins of all mankind."

I felt shame. His words brought my own guilt to the surface, guilt for things I might have said or should have done. I cried out, "What do you expect of me, Lord? What can I do?"

He answered, "Follow me, and I will be with thee, even unto the end of the world."

Again, the sound of Christ's voice was unforgettable, not like any voice I'd ever heard. It was many things all at once. It was commanding, yet emotional, deeply moving to anyone who heard it.

My whole inner self–my soul–was uplifted by His words. I wept some more. A gush of tears streamed from my eyes, down my face. I didn't know it then, but this was the first step in my being born anew.

Out of nowhere, I felt a sympathetic hand upon my shoulder, comforting me. I jerked around, staring into the face of the compassionate young man I had seen earlier in the crowd. On the ground close beside me, he observed, "I saw you crying."

I couldn't hold my feelings back, "How can they do this to Him?"

"They don't know He's the Son of God–but you–you seem to know it."

"Yes, I've always known it." I hesitated looking into the face of this kind, understanding young man. I had to ask, "How is it you know Jesus?"

"I'm called young John because I'm the youngest of those who follow Him. But you should follow Him as well. He's dying for all of our sins."

"Beyond this death," I told him, "He will soon sit down at the right hand of the throne of God."

This got young John's attention. I felt his eyes carefully studying me as he expressed his gratitude, "Bless you for saying that, but just how do you know? Who are you?"

I answered, "I'm someone who knows He's our Lord and Savior."

Just then, both John and I looked up as Christ's breathing became louder and more labored. I think Jesus knew the limits of what the human body could take. An expression of love formed on His face as He looked at both of us, whispering, "I will be with you always." A brief moment of silence passed as he summoned up a final gasp of human life, declaring, "It is finished."

In response, to make sure of this, a Roman soldier standing nearby stepped forward with a long spear, plunging it into His side. Withdrawing it, both blood and water gushed from the gaping wound.

On his knees, tears in his eyes, powerful words of truth came from young John's heart, "He has died so mankind might have forgiveness."

Shaking with emotion, I looked up at Jesus and cried, "My Lord and my God." Crawling forward, touching the base of the cross, the blood from His wounds streamed down over my hands, completely covering them. Focusing on my hands now, I realized what Jesus had done, "He has washed away my sins with His blood."

Almost immediately, one could sense the anger of God about to explode. Clouds seemed to form rapidly and spread across the clear sky above the cross. The world around Golgotha Hill was plunged into unreal darkness at mid-day.

From a deadly quiet, the earth began to rumble with a quaking fury. Amidst crashes of thunder, lightning tore across the horizon, growing closer to us by the second.

An expression of fear formed on a battle-hardened Roman soldier's face. He blurted out, "It's the wrath of God!" Indeed, it really was, for it was His son who had just given up his life in payment for our sins.

Young John was close enough that I could hear him above the growing tumult. "The Lord's judgment will be upon all of them! They have sinned a great sin!"

Powerful, almost gale-force winds became ever louder as they approached. Surging across the entire landscape, I felt surrounded by them. Smashing into my face with such tremendous force, my hair was whipped back in a mass of wild confusion. I was pelted by sheets of rain which were beginning to hit me with increasing force. At the same time, blinding flashes of lightning were coming closer to my face.

Shutting my eyes to the storm's fury, I crouched low on the ground. Then all went silent for a long moment. I opened my eyes slowly. I suddenly awakened from a dream. Only it was no dream.

Looking around, I found myself back in the quiet of the chapel. I was on the floor in front of the altar. Even though I had returned to the present, the images of 2,000 years ago were still running through my mind. Those images were seared into my memory.

Profoundly shaken, I rose to my feet, bracing myself

against the altar table. Turning around, I walked back up the center aisle a few rows and sat down. In my head, I tried to review what had just happened. I asked myself, was it a vision? I knew in my heart I had actually been to another place in a far-off time.

Sitting there, I could feel the healing power of Jesus. I whispered aloud, "After ten years of darkness, God has let a ray of light shine into my life."

I had thought I was alone in the chapel. I did not realize there was another pair of ears listening to me. From out of the shadows, a voice spoke up "Whether you know it or not, the Lord wanted you to come in here."

I asked, "Who are you?"

The voice answered, "One who can help you."

# CHAPTER 5

# Sister Mary

From where I was sitting, once again, something shining from within the cross at the altar got my attention. In awe, I whispered, "Oh God, thank you for having mercy upon my soul."

From the voice behind me came another comment, "Of course, my child. Christ shed His precious blood so that you might have forgiveness of your sins."

I looked around behind me, trying to pinpoint the source of those words. I could see no one within the deep shadows of the dimly lit chapel. But the voice came from behind me. So I got up and started walking back toward the chapel entrance. Reaching the last few rows, I sat down in one of the aisle seats.

No one appeared to be in the chapel but me. Then as I leaned forward with clasped hands to pray, I heard a nearby voice say, "It's time for us to meet." The voice came from just a few seats over, in the same row I was in.

I glanced over to see a white-haired woman smiling at me. Though elderly, she had a youthful sparkle around her eyes. There was a friendly manner about her as she spoke, "Hello, I'm Sister Mary."

"I'm Naomi Larson. I didn't see you sitting there." In truth, though, it was as if she had just materialized out of the darkness.

Only a couple of seats separated us, so we began to talk. I asked, "How is it that you're here?"

"Even though I'm called 'Sister Mary,' I'm not a nun. As you can see, I'm not dressed as a nun." Indeed, she wore a casual pull-over sweater and slacks. She explained, "I'm here because I founded *All Souls Hospice* almost twenty years ago. I keep coming back because there's so much good I can do here. I saw you praying, and somehow I knew I could help you."

"Yes, I wanted to talk to Jesus and pray for His help."

"Whatever people think of Him, Jesus was the one who changed the entire course of human history. His sacrifice on the cross has brought salvation to all mankind."

"I was seeking Him at your altar when I saw a light around the cross there."

"It was His light you saw, the light of the world. It's the light of hope that consoles all who need Him. When Jesus said, *I am with you always*, He meant if you call on Him as you did at the altar, His spirit will be here to help you."

"I certainly need His help now. I've been to so many dark places in the past ten years and seen so much wrong in the world. I became disillusioned with life and lost my faith. I am ashamed of that. I need God's help to sort things out, to help me."

"Naomi, God has placed knowledge in our brains, ideas of right and wrong to live by. It is only when individuals allow themselves to be corrupted by evil, do they commit sin. As you know, the greatest sin ever committed by the mind of man was the crucifixion of Jesus Christ."

"It was the greatest sin ever done."

"How do you know that, my child?"

"I know that because I was there. When I came in here to pray, I was caught up in a vision when I touched the cross at your altar. Somehow, I was transported back two thousand years and saw the crucifixion of Christ. Every detail of what happened unfolded before my very eyes. I know that sounds impossible, but…."

"It's not impossible," insisted Sister Mary, interrupting me. "Nothing is impossible if the Lord wants it to be so. There are so many things in Heaven and Earth that we do not understand or could even comprehend."

I conceded, "I did feel like I was there." Still unsure of what I saw, I added, "Yet it could've been some sort of strange vision."

"Naomi, are you so sure it was just a vision? Look at the

palms of your hands where you crawled over the sharp rocks of Golgotha Hill."

I glanced down at my hands. They were scabbed and still bleeding. The realization of this truth left me shaking. I reached out for answers from Sister Mary, "Then somehow what happened to me was real?"

Sister Mary explained it this way, "Time is all relative to a God of infinite power. What happened two thousand years ago is only a few seconds to our Lord."

"But why? Why was I there?"

"God works in mysterious ways, but to Him, there is a purpose for everything that happens."

"But what purpose could involve me? I've done nothing special in my life."

"God knows everything about you, everything that has happened and will happen. Something will happen in your life, something that you have not yet done, that will make you very special to the Lord."

"I wish that could be true. But in this whole world, I feel so insignificant."

"My child, throughout all history, God has chosen those that seem insignificant to be special. He chose David, a simple shepherd boy, to be King over Israel. He made Jesus, the son of a lowly carpenter, to be a King of Kings, and change the world. He took Peter, a simple fisherman, and made him a fisherman of men and one of the founders of His church."

"I could never hope to be like any of them."

"What most people don't realize is that God has a plan for all of us if we open up our hearts to Him. You may not know it, but God is actively involved in your life. You have a destiny. If you continue to open up your heart to Him as you did at our altar, the Lord will illuminate your future for you. He will share His light—the light of the world—with you."

As we talked, she helped me to understand things. She had answers to my every question. She believed everything that happened to me.

Then I asked her, "What do you think? Why am I here right now?"

Sister Mary told me what she thought, "I believe the Lord brought you here for a reason so that we could talk. Through your faith, you have acknowledged God. In your vision, you acknowledged Jesus as your Lord and Savior. Now you need to open up your whole heart and soul to Him. My child, He wants to have a relationship with you, making you anew as He guides you, walking His pathway, the pathway of God."

I knew in my heart she was right and confessed, "I feel His presence even now."

"And well, you should. This is His chapel, His house. It is for His children."

"I want to be one of His children."

"You already are. We are all God's children. Every human being has His seed. It's planted inside your soul. It's His greatest gift, the gift of life. God's spark made your soul come alive, turning you into a living, breathing human being."

"How shall I serve the Lord and be worthy of Him? What do you think God wants me to do now?"

"I sense you're very close to discovering that yourself. When Jesus spoke to you from the cross, He wanted you to take up His work and follow Him. Reach deep into your mind and heart, and think about the truth of what I'm about to say: Jesus wants you to stay here and serve Him within these walls."

"How so?"

"By comforting the souls of those who are in their final days upon this earth."

"You mean those about to die?" Thinking of my mother, I blurted out, "Death is so final!"

"Don't you think that," contradicted Sister Mary, continuing, "Death is just the beginning of a beautiful journey. From the ashes of death, our souls will rise up to meet the Lord in Heaven."

Her words spoke to my soul. I wanted them to be true. Words came from my heart, "I want to believe you."

"Naomi, at this very moment, you are desperately needed in the work at *All Souls*."

I looked up into Sister Mary's face and saw someone caught up in the passion of her work. I felt like I was in the presence of someone who possessed an aura that was far greater than any human being I'd ever met. Just looking at her made me realize this woman was a force of nature. I was suddenly filled with admiration for her. I asked, "Sister Mary, what happened in your life to make you the person you are?"

"Like you, it was an encounter with Jesus that changed my life. One day, many years ago, He knocked at the door of my soul, wanting me to let Him in."

"What happened?"

"He filled me with His wisdom and spirit. Over time, He charged me with the task of founding this hospice. I tell you, Naomi, there is nothing to compare with having God as your co-pilot in life."

Listening to her, feeling the passion and sincerity that was inside her filled me with similar enthusiasm. It was electric. A sort of spiritual awakening took hold of me. I knew something more clearly than any other time in my entire life. "I want to be like you," I told her. "I want the Lord inside me too!"

"If you do, it will change your life forever. Having the spirit of the Lord inside you will teach you something that most people don't know."

"What's that?"

"When you touched the cross, you realized the Son of God is not of this world. Two thousand years ago, when Pilate asked Jesus, 'Are you the King of the Jews?', Christ answered, *My kingdom is not of this world.* Jesus resides in the spiritual realm and in the hearts of all who welcome Him into themselves."

I asked, not quite understanding, "Jesus is in the spiritual realm?"

"This is what many do not understand. Spiritual energy is not visible to the human eye. This is why the Spirit world–Heaven and the hereafter–is invisible to mortal man. At this point in time, man, with all his scientific knowledge of quantum physics, is still only in the rudimentary stages of even beginning to understand the Creator and His creation of all life billions of years ago. God made life to extend far beyond this life on Earth. It's actually in two realms. We are beings of flesh and blood, living in the physical realm. Beyond death, there is the spiritual realm. It's where Jesus and the souls of the faithful reside."

"I think I'm beginning to understand."

"In time, He wants you to give those who enter *All Souls* a message."

"What message?"

"That upon death they will stand before the throne of Jesus in the spiritual realm."

Sister Mary's vast knowledge and wisdom was so much more than others. I had to ask, "How is it you know so much?"

"I know all that I'm telling you because God has spoken to my heart. My knowledge comes from the Holy Spirit."

"The Holy Spirit?"

"It is the spirit of God. It's in this chapel, all around us, everywhere on Earth, all at once at the same time. This spirit lingers around everything His spiritual hand has ever touched throughout the universe. The Holy Spirit is at the very center of all existence since the beginning of time."

Trying to wrap my head around what she was saying, I reacted, "It's almost frightening when one begins to think about it."

"My child, be not afraid. The Lord is a loving God. He knows all, even the hurt from the loss of your mother, that still exists inside your soul. Let your heart be no longer troubled. Accept the Lord's healing hand."

Even as she spoke, emotion welled up within me, and tears formed in my eyes. At the same time, I felt a powerful surge of faith inside myself, like nothing I had ever experienced in my entire life. I whispered, "Thank you, Sister Mary, for helping me, but how?"

"How do I know so much? I know more about you than you could ever dream. That's why I'm here, to help you."

"Are you an angel?"

"Some have said that. Some have called me a human angel, a spirit, even a ghost. Perhaps I'm a bit of all three. You decide, whatever name you're comfortable with suits me fine."

"I think I'll call you my guardian angel."

"Bless you for that, Naomi."

"If indeed you are my guardian angel, what should I do next?"

"Out front, in the lobby, there is a job posting for a

position here. Our Chaplain, Stephen Andrews, needs an assistant."

"I know you mean well, but a chaplain's assistant. I know I don't have the qualifications for such a position."

"Naomi, the one thing you should remember is that through God, all things are possible."

"Yes, I'll try to remember." Once more, she had told me something that would help me. That is, I should stay strong in my faith, never losing it.

"Now listen to me," she said, getting my full attention, "Stephen Andrews is a good man and a friend of mine. On your way out, indulge me. Go see him and talk with him anyway. If he doubts you, tell him Sister Mary sent you. Tell him you talked to me in the chapel. He will understand. Please promise you will do this for me."

I avoided her searching eyes for a moment, looking down. I knew I had to do it. How could I turn down someone so close to God? Giving in, I assured her, "Okay, for my guardian angel, I'll talk to Chaplain Andrews. I promise."

Looking up, I wanted to see her approval, but Sister Mary was gone. Had she left without making a sound? My eyes scanned the entire chapel. There was no sign of her anywhere. She had completely vanished. Words escaped my lips, "Where did you go?"

To my astonishment, even though she was physically gone, her voice responded, "I'm still here. Naomi, from this day forward, never lose your faith in the Lord. Remember, the doorway that will lead you to God is inside yourself. Listen to His voice, and you will begin a journey that will take you all the way to eternity's gate."

Hearing those words, a strange feeling of belonging came over me. A feeling that the Lord wanted me here lingered inside my head. Perhaps, I was home.

Complete silence filled the chapel as I left. Alone with my thoughts, I realized I had just talked with an angel. Indeed, she was my guardian angel.

# CHAPTER 6

# Decisions

Reaching the chapel doors, I thought, most people have never seen a ghost, let alone talked to one. Actually, though, she was my guardian angel.

Sister Mary was part of my salvation. After my encounter with her, I felt closer to God than I had ever been.

This chapel had become a healing place for all my sorrows. If one has been broken by verbal or physical abuse, or anything encountered during one's life, God is there if you seek Him. All that had lingered with me the past ten years was beginning to heal. Inner peace was taking its place.

I had felt the power of our Lord through a vision. He had extended the hand of hope into my life and saved my soul. In a way that is beyond human understanding, He was still helping me.

A new awareness of how much God is involved in our

lives rose up within me. He was telling me to listen to my heart. *All Souls Hospice* was a good place where I could become someone of worth and value to others. If I stayed here, my life would find a new beginning. Leaving the chapel, back in the hallway, I stood there thinking about what was a miracle to me. I was in a place where I was communicating with Jesus Christ. Regaining my lost faith, I had found redemption at the foot of the cross of Jesus. I was now ready to dedicate the rest of my life to the Lord.

I realized something more clearly than ever before. Within the hearts of people of faith, there is a dwelling place for the spirit of the Lord. God gives a chance for redemption to anyone who seeks it. His spirit is there–always there–if we welcome it into ourselves.

The knowledge gained from my vision, together with what I'd learned from Sister Mary, had helped me. What all mankind thirsts for, a greater knowledge and closeness to God, was within my grasp.

I'd made my decision. I wanted to open the doorway within my own soul and welcome Him into my life. I whispered, "I am ready, Lord. Please dwell within me."

Almost immediately, something was happening. I heard His voice speak to my mind. *I will come and abide within you.*

I froze, not moving at all, fully recognizing this was the voice of Jesus, the same one I heard from the cross in my vision. I answered, "Please, Lord, I so need the benefit of your wisdom in my life."

The Voice replied, *I will instruct and teach you in what you should do.* It was just as Sister Mary had said. The spirit of the Lord would be with me, guiding me every step of the way.

My mind was opening up to a new world. My sight and hearing were taking in so much more. God's spirit was expanding my mind, helping me to see the world as I'd never seen it.

It became clear to me that I had been walking in darkness for the past ten years. But now, I was walking in the light–the light of God.

Something holy and sacred was becoming part of me. It was something spiritual that comes from the river that flows by the throne of God. My body and soul were being cleansed by the presence of God's spirit. I was being born again, becoming a new person, a better person than I'd ever been. I was becoming one with the Lord. I felt His presence guiding me in what He wanted me to do.

The voice of Sister Mary spoke to my mind, "As the strength of your faith continues to grow, you will become someone greater than you could ever imagine. Remember what I've told you, He knows everything you are capable of doing and everything you will become."

Walking back up the long hallway to the chaplain's office, every step I took was with greater confidence. I could feel His presence leading me into a new future.

Standing in front of the closed door to the chaplain's

office, I knew I was here for His purpose. All things would work together for good. With the spirit of the Lord in my life, I knew His light would illuminate the path my journey would take.

I could see meaning and purpose coming back into my life. New energy circulating throughout my body was supporting me. It was the essence of the Holy Spirit.

Inside my mind and heart, I knew this was the first day of my new life as a child of God within *All Souls Hospice*. I had made my decision to keep my promise and talk with Chaplain Andrews. I felt like everything that was about to happen was meant to be. I was beginning to accept that this place was going to be my new home.

After what happened in the chapel, I had a lot of questions for Stephen Andrews. Knocking on the chaplain's door, his voice answered from within, "Come in."

# CHAPTER 7

# Revelations

As I entered and seated myself in a chair in front of Chaplain Andrews' desk, his eyes followed me, studying me closely. Seated directly across from me, he was welcoming, "Ms. Naomi, I'm so glad you decided to stop by and see me. You know," he hesitated for a moment, then added, "there's something about you that reminds me of someone I once knew."

"Chaplain Andrews," I interrupted, "I have several questions I think you might be able to answer. When I entered your chapel, I encountered something I can't explain, something all-powerful. What do you think it was?"

"I know what it was. The power of the Lord was getting inside you, working its way into your soul so that it might show you some things."

"Yes," I explained, "I had a vision, but it was like nothing I've ever seen or felt. In it, I saw Jesus. Somehow on a level beyond human understanding, I had been plunged into the reality of 2,000 years ago. It was like a miracle. I believe you knew much more about your chapel than you let on before I went through those doors."

"If I told you before, would you have believed me? What happened to you in our chapel was not like a miracle. IT WAS a miracle. The Lord wanted to get inside you, to see if you were ready to be transformed, to be used by Him in His work."

"How is it that you know this, Chaplain?"

"Because the same thing happened to me when I first came here as a young chaplain, almost twenty years ago. Call it a feeling or a premonition. I just knew the Lord wanted to help you. Now, He will be there for you always."

I explained further, "After I came out of my vision, I spoke to someone in your chapel, someone I now believe was an angel."

"I don't doubt you. I believe you far more than you know. I think there are more guardian angels in this world than most people realize. You see, I have a guardian angel as well, one that helps me in my work here at *All Souls*."

"You do?"

"I even happen to have a photograph of her here on my desk." Picking up the framed picture that was facing him, Chaplain Andrews turned it around, so the image was clearly visible from where I was sitting. "This is her," he added.

"This is my angel."

Recognizing her right away, her name escaped my lips, "Sister Mary! This is who I spoke to in the chapel just a few minutes ago!"

"I'm not surprised," confessed Chaplain Andrews. "There have been multiple sightings of her spirit. Some say her ghost, for the last seven years, since the day of her passing."

"At first, I wasn't sure," I observed. "She seemed so real. She knew so much about everything and everyone."

"She was a remarkable woman. If I may, I'd like to tell you more about her."

"I'd like to hear it," I said, having a feeling it would be just as much his story as it was her story.

"It was many years ago," he began, "when I first met Mary Sullivan." As he started, I glanced down at the photo of a much younger Stephen Andrews, twenty years younger, with Sister Mary looking remarkably unchanged from when I saw her in the chapel less than an hour ago.

"Mary was a founding member of the Sisters of Mercy order, over at the state capital. Even then," Chaplain Andrews continued, "Mary had this vision of establishing a hospice for those in their last days of life. Through her force of will, she obtained the necessary public funding, and *All Souls Hospice* was born."

Glancing at the photograph of them together, I asked, "How did you meet her?"

"I had just graduated from a seminary and was in the process of being ordained when Sister Mary took me under her wing, agreeing to let me serve my internship as her chaplain at *All Souls*. Even as a young man, I was a very spiritual person."

"And so was she?"

"Oh yes, even then. When we first met, it was like a meeting that was destined to happen. She always said that God intends for some people to meet in this life so they might inspire each other's lives. I believe that because it was through Sister Mary, I have made my work here my life's work. And you know something?"

"What?"

"I've never regretted it."

Feeling his sincerity, I added, "At one time or another, we all need someone to help show us the way in our lives. I can tell that she has deeply influenced your life."

"Just knowing her," he revealed, "I saw her becoming God-like in everything she did in her daily life. She was wrapped up in her work here, believing in the good she was doing for those in their final days."

"Meeting her as I did in the chapel, I could tell she was a good person."

In a voice that had known her for many years, he added, "Every day I could see the love of Jesus in her face. Her whole life was dedicated to passing on His message to a world that needs it now more than ever. I miss her so very much."

"She's not gone. Remember, I visited with her spirit in the chapel just in the last hour. You said her spirit is still here within these walls."

"Oh yes, I'm quite sure."

"Didn't you say she was your guardian angel?"

"Yes, I still feel like she is. But I only hear her voice rarely now, sometimes very infrequently. When I said I missed her, it's her physical presence I miss. Very few have only caught a fleeting glimpse of her. None have actually talked to her. Yet, you have spoken to her at length. There has to be a reason. Why?"

"Chaplain Andrews, why do you think she's still here?"

Thinking about my question for a moment, he answered, "When her body was dying, she said her great regret was leaving so much of her work here undone. I believe her spirit just couldn't seem to let go of this place, at least not until she considers her work done."

"The more she talked to me in the chapel, I got the increasing feeling I was talking to a spirit angel, sent from God. You said there had to be a reason she spoke to me. I believe I know the reason. She said you needed help."

"She said I needed help?"

"Yes, she did."

A heaven-sent light seemed to form on the face of Stephen Andrews as he revealed his thoughts, "It's true, I do need help here at *All Souls*. When she was alive, Sister Mary helped me to know and understand what the Lord wanted me to do." He paused for a moment, his eyes studying me closely again. "Naomi, I believe you're truly blessed. I see it clearly now. God has a purpose for you."

He saw something inside me that I was not yet quite sure of. I wondered, thinking back, "Sister Mary said something like that. You think so, too?"

"I must ask you, how did you feel after you left the chapel?"

"A most wonderful feeling filled me. I feel like I've been reborn."

"If that be true," Chaplain Andrews concluded, "then you have to admit something else to yourself."

I didn't have to ask. Searching myself, I admitted the truth. "Something of the spirit of God is inside me now. I just know it." I took a deep breath and smiled. "I feel liberated telling someone else."

Chaplain Andrews stood up and came around his desk. Getting closer, sitting in the vacant chair next to me, he closed his hand around mine. "I'll say it again, bless you, Naomi. I see it in your eyes and feel it in the touch of your hand. It doesn't happen often, but it's happened to you. The presence of the Holy Spirit is inside you."

"Then it's happened just as Sister Mary said it would. She told me that and much more. I would truly like to speak to her again."

"I hope it works out that you can. Try to remember, though. You will be speaking to what is her spiritual essence.

As such, she is a step closer to the Lord than we are. I think she was heaven-sent to meet you for a purpose."

"I wonder about that. Why me?"

"Most of us never know why God picks us. Even Moses did not know why God picked him to lead a nation out of bondage thousands of years ago. I often ask myself, why am I here? I believe you're here because He sees something in you. Perhaps it's a capacity for good that will benefit others. If you and I can help just one other person, I believe we will have done good in the sight of the Lord."

Chaplain Andrews' words reached into my heart and lifted me up. I was sincerely moved, "I want to be the person you speak of or at least try to be that person."

"You will be that person." There was such strength and authority in Stephen Andrews' voice. He had just given me a morale booster that gave me a new feeling of confidence in myself.

My whole belief system was evolving. My mind was opening up, accepting new ideas. "You know, Chaplain, until today, I wasn't quite sure if I believed in spirits or angels."

"Throughout history, in both the Old and New Testaments, there are recorded appearances of spirits and angels. Jesus went up into the mountains where He received the advice and counsel from the spirits of Moses and Elijah."

"Yes, I have read those stories, but I have still wondered, how is it possible for spirits to appear before mortal man?"

"The power of Almighty God makes all things possible.

I know this to be true because, like you, I have seen and talked to the spirit of Sister Mary myself."

Accepting what he was saying, my thoughts came to a conclusion, "There is so much we don't know."

"You're right, Naomi. There's a lot out there we mortals don't know or could even begin to comprehend. There are so many things beyond our own human existence that are of the Lord: the possibility of eternal life and what lies beyond our own little world in multiple galaxies. Then there is the question of Heaven itself."

"Where is Heaven? What do you think?" I was eager to know his opinion.

"Perhaps the power of God, His angels and spirits, and what we call Heaven, is existing on spiritual plains that we cannot see, even with the aid of our most powerful telescopes. It all boggles the mind. But there is one thing we do know if our faith is strong enough."

"Stephen, what is the one thing we all know?"

"Those that do not have closed minds know God IS real. It is through faith that all things are possible. If we open up our hearts and minds to Him, He will show us the way, guiding us through this life and beyond."

"Stephen, you have the faith you speak about."

"Yes, with all my heart, I do."

"You still believe the spirit of Sister Mary is here?"

"Now, more than ever, I feel her presence in this building."

"Then will you ask her if I'm here to help you in your work?"

He thought for a moment, then answered, "I no longer need to ask her. She knew I needed an assistant. Sister Mary is the reason I've stayed on here, and she is the reason I'm going to ask you to stay if you will, Ms. Naomi."

I felt like the words Sister Mary said to me in the chapel were coming true, like from a prophecy of what was going to happen. I wanted to keep the promise I'd made to her and to our Lord. Thinking about it, I knew this was my destiny, as I answered, "Stephen, I will stay, but on one condition."

"What is that?"

"If we are going to work closely together, we should support each other."

"Yes, of course," he agreed.

"Then please, Stephen, just call me 'Naomi,' not Ms. Naomi."

A smile formed on his face as he took my hand, "I promise, Naomi."

# CHAPTER 8

# Of Life And Death

A sustained rain had been going on somewhere in the distance but was now over. A rainbow had formed in the sky and stretched in the form of an arc along the horizon.

"Some call it a phenomenon; others call it a miracle." Chaplain Andrews was commenting on what we saw from the window within his office.

"I thought it had greater significance in the Bible."

"You're right, Naomi. In Genesis, a rainbow is the sign of the covenant God made with Noah and every living creature that survived the flood. God promised the earth would never again be consumed by water."

"Then God shows His compassion and love for all people of faith through His rainbows?"

"That's true, but even more so when He sent His Son to be our savior. I think about the sacrifice Jesus made on the cross. He took unto himself the punishment for the sins of all mankind so that we might receive redemption and the gift of eternal life in Heaven. It's God's promise to all of us through His Son, Jesus Christ."

"From the time of Noah to the time of Jesus, I see something very clearly now. It's God's light shining through the darkness, protecting us from whatever threatens to consume our lives. It's like a covenant, God's love for people of faith down through the ages."

"Now we come to you, Naomi, and why God has come to you."

"What do you mean?"

"Because of what happened to you in our chapel, I think the Lord is making a covenant with you, with this rainbow. I believe God rules the world in ways most humans don't understand."

"What I learned in the chapel from Sister Mary has helped me to understand how much God is all around us. She helped me see that this is a place of miracles and that you are doing God's work here. Stephen, she said you needed someone to help you, to be your assistant. I didn't think I was qualified, but she made me believe that you would accept me anyway."

"I do accept you. I'll help you, Sister Mary's spirit will help you, and God will help you. So, let's start here and now."

"Yes, let's start right now, in front of your office window."

"Very well," Stephen smiled, reacting to my enthusiasm.

He began, "I'm going to tell you about what I've learned. As human beings, our lives have a beginning and an end. Between these two points, our lives have an arc that carries us from our childhood through our middle years and then to our final time on earth. It's here, in *All Souls Hospice*, we see those worn-out bodies living out their final days. As death approaches, most of them will look to us for help in finding inner peace. Looking into their faces, giving each one of them a cup of kindness, is where I'll need your help the most."

"Yes, Stephen, I'll be here to do just that. I'm embracing a calling from the Lord to be here and help you any way I can."

Taking my hand again, he spoke from his heart, "Your commitment means the world to me."

I asked, "How was it for you when you first came here?"

"Right off, with Sister Mary's help, I began studying man's mortal end on this earth and what happens afterward."

"What happens afterward?"

"Death of the physical body is not the end, but rather the beginning of a journey of the human consciousness to a higher state in the spiritual realm. As a person of faith and a Christian, I have come to believe it."

I agreed, "From just what I've seen and learned today, I believe it too."

Stephen's searching eyes looked inside me, evaluating me, "What we do here sometimes takes on a life of its own. It might even consume what free time you may have."

"I am prepared for just such a sacrifice. I will give up every second of my private life doing what the Lord wants me to do. I believe God brought me here for that very purpose. At the cross in my vision, this is what my Savior charged me with. Can I do less than what He has done for me?"

"Naomi, may the Good Lord bless you in your covenant with Him."

"If I can help the terminally ill within these walls, even in a small way, I'll feel like I'm doing what the Lord would have me do."

Stephen truly accepted me in that moment, "I believe God put us both here for a reason, perhaps to help each other. I think everyone in the world serves a purpose according to His all-encompassing will."

Turning from the window, we walked across the room, stopping in front of his office door. Opening it, Stephen hesitated for a moment, then asked me, "Naomi, can you start tomorrow morning?"

I answered, "I can start anytime." I explained further, "I just came in on the bus this very morning. Once here, I had no previous plans or obligations. Though I'm originally from Holdenville, I've been gone for over ten years. I no longer know anyone here."

Stephen became curious, "If I may ask, then why did you come back here?"

I told him the truth, "One night, I heard the voice of my late mother, urging me to come back here. She was such a good person of faith. I had always taken her advice to heart, so I thought about it. Some say a place is always inside you. Then I started feeling something was drawing me back here. That's when I decided to act upon my feelings."

"I'm glad you came back."

"I was in a pretty bad place when I left the west coast. I've only got the clothes on my back and very little money in my pocket after I bought my bus ticket. Coming back to Holdenville was a real act of faith on my part."

"Sometimes life takes us to unexpected places, but always brings us to where we should be. As my assistant, in addition to a salary, I can offer you free room and board in the vacant quarters just down the hall."

"I don't know what to say."

"You don't have to say anything."

Following Stephen out into the long hall, we stopped on down from his office, in front of a closed door. I noticed it was only a few feet from the double doors leading into the chapel.

"Beyond this door," Stephen continued, "are the quarters for our new chaplain's assistant, which would be you."

I immediately expressed my gratitude, "I hope I can justify your faith in me."

"Sister Mary has faith in you, and that's good enough for me. Yet, I must tell you, over time, this place will change you."

"Life is full of change. Perhaps it will be for the best.

Anyway, how do you know this?"

"During my years here, I've been witness to many striking things. I've seen what was supposed to be the finality of death become the birth of a new beginning. On the floor above us, I have seen countless deathbed patients experience visions with deceased relatives and friends. Some who had never believed had encounters with angels, or even Jesus."

"It must be inspiring to witness."

"Yes, it's incredibly moving to see those who embrace the Lord in the last days of their lives. They make peace with the world around them. They sometimes even see what is to come beyond this life. A few even get a glimpse into what one might call Heaven. Some told me they had seen a place full of dazzling colors and incredible light, a place none like anything on earth. I believe, as it was for me, it will be a transformative experience for you as well."

"God reached into my soul and brought me here in the first place. If things happen as you have described, my faith will only be strengthened."

Moved by what I said, he reacted, "In all honesty, I speak from my heart. I'm so very glad God brought you here."

Feeling his sincerity, I agreed, "I'm glad too."

Remaining silent, Stephen just nodded as a slight smile formed on his face. I could see he was filled with a good feeling about my presence here. Reaching down, turning the doorknob, he opened the door, saying something that would turn out to be very prophetic, "Welcome to your new home."

As I entered, somehow, even then, I knew the most significant period of my life was ahead of me. The change that Stephen Andrews predicted was about to begin.

# CHAPTER 9

# A Spiritual Presence

Inside my quarters, I soon found that a spiritual presence abided there as well. The Lord's presence filled my room in so many ways, permeating everything there.

With only one brief interruption, I sat there alone all afternoon, thinking about the events of that morning. Chaplain Andrews brought me some food from the upstairs lunch room and some clean caregiver clothes in my size. He also dropped off some necessities for the adjoining bathroom within my quarters.

Sitting on a small sofa, I couldn't escape thinking about Sister Mary. Many questions regarding her ran unceasingly through my mind. Unable to escape her, I went to the bathroom to wash my face and try to clear my head.

Without the benefit of turning on the bathroom light, I splashed my face with cool water. This was only a temporary relief, for suddenly, a glow formed within the mirror above the sink. Coming from an unseen light source, it lit up its surface. As the light grew stronger, an image began to form and take place within the glass. It was blurred and transparent. Yet, with each succeeding second, it was becoming clearer. I could not move. My eyes were riveted to what was happening. As the glow ceased, I stepped backward and was stunned at the clear image of what I saw.

Before me was the transparent image of Sister Mary staring at me from within the mirror, in her soft, almost quiet voice, she spoke to me, "Naomi, I had to see you."

Despite this unusual means of contact, her friendly voice put me at ease. I asked, "What is it, Sister Mary?"

She explained, "I wanted you to know I'm very proud of how well you're getting along with Chaplain Andrews. Stephen is so in need of help, much more than he knows." It was as though she was speaking from another realm of existence. The mirror had become a window to another place. She continued, "I've been observing you since you left the chapel. Naomi, I believe you have the gift."

Knowing I had been speaking to a hallucination, I turned away from the mirror. I stepped into the bathroom doorway. Still curious, though, I whispered back, asking, "What gift?"

"A gift many would like to have." This time her voice came from my room. I looked around and, there was Sister Mary standing directly in front of me. This time she appeared to be in the flesh, like any other normal person. She explained further, "You have the gift of faith and wisdom combined. It is the compassion you have for others that enabled you to experience Christ's crucifixion with such a great feeling. In time, drawing on this same compassion that is within your soul, you will lift the hearts of those who are spending their last days here."

"There is something I have to ask you, Sister Mary. Please don't take offense, but I have to know. Are you real, right here, right now?"

"No offense taken, my child. I prefer to think of myself as the living consciousness of my former self, who stands before you only by the will of Almighty God. You see and hear me as you do because the faith you possess makes me real to your mind. What most people fail to grasp is that through faith, all things are possible."

"Yes, through faith," I agreed, "you're here in my room right now."

"That's true, right now, but," Sister Mary became hesitant as her eyes surveyed the room, then explaining, "You see, this was my room."

"What?" Surprised, I slumped back onto the small sofa that was behind me. "Chaplain Andrews made no mention of it when he offered this room to me."

"Of course not. He didn't want you to think this room might be haunted. My child, I want you to be reassured that I'm not going to haunt you. It just saddens me I can't be here to complete my work. But you're here now. I promise you, that I will no longer appear in this room unless you call on me."

"I may do that, for I still need your advice and counsel."

Glancing over at the nearby bed, Sister Mary remembered, "You know, Mary Sullivan died in that very bed. It was a good bed for me, and I'm sure it will be a good bed for you." The saddened look became more pronounced as she added, "I didn't want to go." Her mind seemed to be full of past memories as she sat down on the sofa beside me.

"There is a reason you're still here," I said, extending a cup of kindness to her. "After all, you're my guardian angel."

"God has allowed me to return here as a spirit. But my work is still unfinished on this earthly plain. So here I am doing what I can on behalf of my Savior as long as He allows me to do so. But, there's only so much a spirit can do."

"Tell me about spirits, Sister Mary. I don't remember reading about them in the Bible."

"Oh, it's there if you look. Go to John, Chapter 3. It says that Heaven is for spiritual beings, that within all of us, our spiritual essence exists. Also, go to 1st Corinthians 15:50 and 2nd Peter 1:18. It says our flesh and blood bodies must return to spirit form before we can enter the Kingdom of Heaven. Answers have been out there for thousands of years for those that want answers to life's mysteries."

I had to ask, "What about Jesus?"

Sister Mary explained, "After His death on the cross,

Jesus came back in spirit form to prove to His apostles that the soul survives the death of the physical body."

"Is that true with everyone?"

"Every person has a soul. It is the essence of who you and I are. Upon the death of our bodies, our souls return to God. The soul is invisible to the human eye, being visible only to God and His Heavenly angels."

"But you can see into my soul."

"Yes, I can. But this is only true because God allows me to do so."

Taking in all that she was saying, I had to admit, "There is so much I don't know, so much I have to learn."

"Naomi, it's important to remember that there are two bodies within each of us. There is a physical body and a spiritual body. In the Bible, read 1st Corinthians, Chapter 15, verses 35 through 44 for more."

Finding myself plunged into Sister Mary's world of answers, I asked her the most profound question of all, "What happens when we die?"

"What I tell you, Naomi is from my own experience. It was only upon the death of my own physical body that I realized, looking down at the lifeless form, I was dead. It was then I discovered the soul separates from the body at the time of its death. I felt the light of God pulling me upward into it. I saw Jesus within the light. He said, *Come unto me, you who labored in my name's sake, and I will give you eternal peace.* But I resisted. Since then, I have remained a spirit within these walls."

I glanced over to thank her for answering my question, but she had completely vanished in a mere fraction of a second. It was as if she had never been there, but of course, I knew better. In the days and months to come, she would always be part of my salvation.

At that moment, though, I was alone again in my room. Glancing around, I saw a Bible sitting on the end table next to the sofa. Picking it up, I started looking up the verses Sister Mary had suggested I read. What started out to be a few minutes drifted into hours. As I absorbed scripture after scripture, I felt my own faith becoming stronger within myself.

As I read, everything was becoming clearer to me, more so than ever before in my life. My mind was opening up to a new level of understanding. It was clear to me now that the mind is the thinking part of the human soul. I felt something happening inside my head. It was as Sister Mary had said: The Holy Spirit was inside me, cleansing me.

I heard the voice of Jesus speak to my mind. *I will make thee anew as my servant.* Hearing His voice made me think about my vision again. For an instant, I was back there looking up at Him as He was on the cross. This time though, I understood Jesus had come into my mind to reveal His truth to me. It was by the shedding of His blood that He paid the price for all our sins. The Son of God so loved us that He became human and died so we might share everlasting life with Him.

I was humbled to my core by these thoughts. He was calling me to serve Him here. I answered that calling, whispering, "I will serve you, Lord, with all my heart and all my soul."

Later that night, as I lay in bed, I prayed for His help and guidance. I formed a mental picture of Jesus in my mind. As I did so, I sensed His presence drawing near to me. In answer to my prayer, I heard Him again, *Don't be afraid, for I am with you. I will help and strengthen you, for I am your God.* A moment later, I felt an aura of His light surround me with its warmth and healing.

Waking up the next morning, fresh energy filled me. I got up, feeling the need to go to the window. Opening the blinds, I looked out to see daylight just beginning to form. Coming over the horizon, the first light of a new day bathed my face.

Suddenly feeling an inner need for her, I called out, "Sister Mary, I know you're still here. I need to talk with you."

"I'm here," her voice immediately answered.

I looked around to see her coming near me by the window. Dressed as she always did, she approached me with a smile on her face. Looking as if she were glad I called for her, she said, "I just knew we would have to talk again."

"After you left," I started telling her, "the presence of the Lord came into this room last night."

"Naomi, I know. I see it in your face. The spirit of Jesus

was here."

"He answered my prayer last night. Since my vision, I've felt His spirit near me. Speaking to my mind, He said, *Behold, I stand knocking at your door. If you open it, I will come in and be with you.* I opened that door."

"Now you feel so differently this morning?"

"Yes, I feel more alive than I have in years. There's so much I want to do to serve Him."

"That's exactly how I felt when I first became a servant of Jesus. His spirit is inside you now. My child, He is the light of the world, a light the world needs now more than ever. Now that light is becoming part of you."

"Sister Mary, can you tell me more about God?"

She did not hold back, telling me what she knew, "He has always been and will always be. His life span is beyond the comprehension of man. The best estimate of human scientists is that the universe is 14 billion years old. Yet God was here before all of this, being the Creator of all things."

"It's hard for me to wrap my mind around what you're telling me."

"Yes, it's hard for mortal man to understand what is immortal. His capacity is so great. His consciousness is limitless. He can be here, and at the same time, billions of miles across the universe."

"In a universe so vast, how can we be more than mere specs in His eyes?"

"There are no boundaries or barriers to the love of God.

What makes us special in His eyes is that we are His creation. We are the children of God. Naomi, you are a child of the Lord, an offspring of His love, as is all humanity."

"I want to be worthy of His love."

"Jesus explained it this way when He said, *The greatest of all things is love, for God IS love.* The Lord wants us to bury hate and love one another for all eternity."

"I want to live the rest of my life the way Jesus would want me to live it."

"For those who acknowledge Him in this life, when they stand before the throne of God in Heaven, He will acknowledge them."

"I want to be one of those who can stand proudly before the throne of God when my time comes."

"You can be. In living life, we should all strive to be better persons, giving of ourselves, being kind and outgoing to others. These are the qualities of human angels. Christ's words told us how to be, *Love thy neighbor as thyself.* Naomi, the Lord, has looked into your soul and seen that you possess these qualities, those of a human angel."

I said what I truly felt in my heart, "I love you, Sister Mary. I thought yesterday that you were a part of my salvation. Now I know it for sure."

It seemed to my eyes that a glowing aura surrounded her face as she responded, "I love you too." Without another word, she became transparent and disappeared into nothingness.

I whispered, "You are truly my guardian angel."

As I dressed, I thought yesterday and this morning had been the beginning of heaven-sent enlightenment for me. I was no longer living in the past but in a glorious new future. I was already feeling good about myself when I heard a knock.

Opening the door, Chaplain Andrews was there. He asked, "Are you ready for a new day?"

"As ready as I'll ever be," I said, welcoming him into my room. I needed to talk with him, so I opened up immediately, "Stephen, I did a great deal of soul-searching last night. I prayed. Sister Mary came to see me. We talked for a long time."

He guessed at what I was getting at, "Then you know this was originally her room?"

"Yes, she told me."

"I didn't know how to tell you," he confessed, explaining, "I thought it might bother you. I'm sorry, I should have been completely honest with you. There is something else."

"Please tell me."

Talking further, he revealed, "Sister Mary once told me she would only leave *All Souls* when she found someone to take her place."

"Wouldn't that be you, Stephen?"

"My work here means the world to me. But I know in my heart it's not me. I think she's been looking for a kindred soul with the same sense of dedication she had when she first came here. Perhaps, it might even be you."

"Oh, please don't say that." Such a thought was overwhelming to me. "It's far too soon to say something like that. There's so much I have yet to learn."

"Not to worry. You're young with a long life ahead of you. If you're God's choice, He will give you the time to become the person He wants you to be."

"Getting back to right now, to be the person you think I might become, where do I begin?"

"You begin right now. Before we go upstairs, I want you to consider something that I already know is part of your character. Draw on the love and compassion that's in your heart. Spiritual nourishment is just as important as medical nourishment. To give someone hope while they are in the process of dying is a miracle unto itself. I believe you have it within yourself to do just that."

"Yes, Stephen, a caring nature to others is already part of my heart and soul."

"I like hearing you say that, for *All Souls Hospice* is much more than a place where the sick and terminally ill live out their last days. It's a place where faith can be restored, and hope can be found."

"As for me, *All Souls* is already much more than a hospice."

As we left my room to go upstairs, something inside me was merging with what the Lord wanted me to be.

# CHAPTER 10

# Becoming A
# Chaplain's Assistant

The first thing I noticed when I woke up today was that the circuits within my brain had opened up to the word of God in a new and fresh way. The teachings of Jesus were reaching into my mind as they had never done before in my life.

I felt the power of God's love reaching deep within me, awakening a compassionate understanding for those whose days were numbered. The words of Jesus spoke to me, saying, *Do unto others as you would have them do unto you.* His spirit was guiding me every step of the way.

I was a work in progress, learning little by little alongside other hospice volunteer workers and caregivers. I watched Stephen carefully, observing how he approached those in his care. I witnessed him giving the terminally ill hope for a future that extended beyond this life. Seeing this, I wanted to absorb Stephen's gift into the person I wanted to be.

During my first week, I learned a lot. Each day I grew more confident, doing what God wanted me to do.

I knew the hand of the Lord was guiding me, showing me how to give hope to dying souls. In doing so, I would be giving from that part of me in which His spirit was residing. I understood that what I was doing was a sacred calling. It would be a lifetime commitment.

Entering my second week of hospice work at *All Souls*, I felt the Lord's hand in everything I did. I was absorbing His words into my mind, embracing something of the Kingdom of God within myself. At the same time, I felt a measure of redemption in becoming a better person than I had ever been.

By the beginning of my third week, Stephen was having me read patients' charts before I met them. Learning about them in this way was like having a window into their minds. So when I actually met the patients Stephen would assign to me, I had a good idea of how best I could help them.

One morning toward the end of the week, Stephen had a word with me before making rounds, "The patient I'm about to introduce you to is one I believe you will be able to best help, much more than me."

"Why do you say that?"

"You both have similar personalities and feelings. Other

than that, I have a strong hunch you will be able to bond well together. This lady is about seventy. Her name is Ruth Wilson."

"What else can you tell me about Ruth?"

"She has no living relatives, save a son about your age. But he's on the other side of the world and can't be here. She's terribly lonely. What she needs now, more than ever, is kindness and support. I believe you're the person who could provide that. Will you help me with her?"

"Of course, I will." Even before I met her, the voice that sometimes would whisper to my mind told me this was something I should do.

Meeting Ruth Wilson would lead to several significant events in my future. Even today, I still feel her influence on my life. But I'm getting ahead of myself, a few more steps down the hall, and Stephen and I were at room 203. He indicated, "This is Ruth's room."

Even before meeting Ruth, I had a positive hunch about her. In hindsight, I believe what was about to happen was what the Lord wanted.

Entering her room, Stephen introduced us, "Ruth, this is the young woman I've been telling you about."

There, before me, in an elevated hospital bed raised to a sitting position, was an obviously weak, almost frail woman of about seventy. Ruth suffered visible breathing difficulties connected to her terminal illness.

Rising above her own suffering, she acknowledged us

with a winning smile forming on her face. Beyond that, she possessed a kind heart, something that drew me to her right away.

"Yes, I'm Chaplain Andrew's new assistant, Naomi Larson," I said, introducing myself. "If I can help you in any way, don't hesitate to call on me."

"You can, right now." Her response was immediate. Then, with a sense of urgency in her voice, she added, "Please stay. I would very much like to visit with you."

Stephen, looking over at me, gave his approval, "Yes, why don't you stay awhile? Ruth could use some company. You can catch up with me later."

Looking directly up at him, she was grateful, "Thank you, Chaplain, this means a lot to me."

"Bless you, Ruth," Stephen replied as he left the room.

Alone now, I moved closer to one side of her hospital bed. In doing so, she was better able to focus on me, searching the features of my face. Recognizing something, Ruth's voice was welcoming, "It is you. I've been waiting for you."

I asked, "What do you mean?"

"A voice told me I would meet someone with an inner light, that I would become very good friends with that person in my last days."

"But how do you know it's me?"

"Because I've been seeing things that nobody else can see."

"You can?" Even as I asked, I thought of the spirits and

visions within *All Souls*. Walking over to a nearby window within the room, streaks of light penetrating through the partially drawn blinds enveloped me. Thoughts rolled through my head as I looked over at Ruth, repeating my question, "You say you can see things?"

"Yes, like the light of the Lord that is bathing you right now. When you first came into my room, I could see you were visibly glowing with the inner light you possess."

I reached over and gently took her hand, admitting, "Yes, it's true."

Tears formed in Ruth's eyes as she revealed, "I've heard others say you have a gift, Naomi."

"What gift do you think I have?"

"I've heard you talk to other patents, and some of them have talked about what you have said."

"And what do they say?"

"That you speak of the Hereafter in detail, that you know what is beyond death in Heaven. So, is that your gift?"

"It's not a gift. I only know what the Lord has revealed to me. It's through His eyes I've seen a glimpse of Heaven."

"May I dare ask, is it beautiful?"

"It's beautiful beyond words."

"Is there a verse from the Bible that would mean something to me right now in my final days?"

"Yes, Ruth, there is. I'm reminded of John 3:16. It says, *For God so loved the world that He gave His only son so that anyone who believes in Him will not perish but have everlasting eternal life."*

Her face took on an apprehensive expression as her next question was forming inside her mind. She was already becoming afraid as she asked, with fear in her voice, "What will happen to me when I die?"

Sitting down in the chair next to Ruth's bed, I did my best to reassure her, answering what the spiritual energy within me inspired me to say, "Your soul, the part of you that is eternal spirit, will depart your body and go with the One who is the light of the world. Then you will pass through eternity's gate with Him and stand before the throne of His Father in Heaven."

"Naomi, I do want what you say to be true. I so wish I could have the relationship with Christ that I see you have."

"You can. All you have to do is open up your heart to Him. Acknowledge Him as your Savior. Welcome His Spirit within yourself. Then He will be with your soul, guiding you forever."

"Is it possible? Will Jesus love me?"

"Yes, Ruth, Jesus possesses unconditional love for you and all of humanity."

My conversation with Ruth went on for the rest of the morning. I stayed with her, holding her hand until she was peacefully asleep, taking a nap.

Leaving room 203, I glanced back at her, knowing she was going to be in my prayers that night. Ruth's soft voice and gentle ways had already worked their way into my heart.

Later that evening, returning to my room, I met Chaplain Andrews in the first-floor hallway. He talked about Ruth and my interaction with her, "Naomi, your faith became the best medicine Ruth Wilson could receive. You lifted her up spiritually as no one else could. She truly needed you today."

"I'm glad I could. Her health is so precarious."

"Yes, I wish it weren't so, but the doctors tell me her life expectancy can be numbered in weeks. Ruth is suffering from respiratory failure. It doesn't help matters that she suffered a severe bout with pneumonia less than a year ago. Her already weakened lungs have been made worse. The walls of her heart are becoming like paper."

I sympathized out loud, "She needs all the love and care we can give her. Before I left her, she asked me if I would come back tomorrow."

Stephen understood immediately, "Before anything else, I want you to go see her in the morning. The message you're giving Ruth is exactly the reason you're needed here."

"Stephen, it'll be a message that will lift her up with positive thoughts."

"I'm sure it will," he said, once more believing in me. Then, almost as an afterthought, he asked, "Oh, by the way, how do you like becoming a chaplain's assistant?"

"I like it," I said, answering from my heart, "because I'm doing what the Lord called me to do."

# CHAPTER 11

# A Message Of Hope

Iwould be spending another morning with Ruth Wilson, giving her a message full of hope. The night before, I prayed that God would fill me with the right words to say. From the moment I stuck my head in the door, I knew what they would be. I smiled and said, "It's me!"

"Oh, please, come in!" She seemed overjoyed. Although she was the same frail woman of yesterday, there was a glimmer of hope on her face. I could feel something positive breaking through as she added, "You said you would. I just wasn't sure you really meant it. But you came back."

"Of course, I did. I keep my promises, Ruth."

"I will trust you completely from now on." The doubt in her began to disappear as she opened up. It seemed as though she was inviting me into her life, and even more so, into her heart.

"Naomi, I can see the light of the Lord in your face. You have very penetrating eyes. It's though you're looking directly into my soul."

"I only see what God lets me see."

"I feel like I can tell you anything."

"You can." The words came out of me almost automatically, for I knew I would keep her most personal thoughts confidential. I told her so, "Anything you say to me will remain between us."

She asked, "What would you like to know?"

"If I may ask, how is it that you are here, Ruth?"

"I didn't want to die alone at home. In order for me to get hospice care, my doctor declared I would not survive more than the next six months. My lungs are weak, deteriorating. I have acute respiratory failure. Death is inevitable." This very thought caused her to pause for a moment, but quickly pulling herself together, she continued, "I just hope and pray I will have the courage to face what's to come."

"You're leaving out something."

"What?"

"You will have love and strength that I will bring to the table to support you." Gently taking her hand, I kissed it.

Tears formed in Ruth's eyes. Deeply moved, her words filled with emotion as she told me, "You're a good person."

"Ruth, what about your family?"

A sad look spread over her face, revealing that she was holding onto a lot of inner heartbreak. I quickly said, "That's okay, you don't have to talk about it."

"No, no," she objected, "I want to talk about my past, especially with you, for you're a caring soul."

"Just tell me whatever you feel comfortable telling me." As I tried to reassure her, I could feel a bond of friendship forming between us. Sitting down in the chair by her bed, I listened with an understanding heart as she told me the story of her life.

She talked about the inner heartbreak of her past, "My husband, my parents, my sister, and brother, I watched as they all passed away. With each one, a little part of me also died." Going silent for a moment, she was still feeling their loss.

At the same time, for a few fleeting seconds, I could see inside her past. I had a vision of a younger Ruth raising a small boy, reading the Bible to him. Back in the present, tears were forming in her eyes as she was about to cry.

"No, don't," I pleaded, getting her attention. "I just saw something. I had a vision of you raising a small boy."

"I knew you could see things!" Her voice was excited, my vision getting her complete attention. "What you saw was completely true. After my husband died, I raised our little son to become a good man. He's now a sergeant in the army, serving in Afghanistan. There's so much I would like to tell him, but I know I'll be gone long before he's able to return home."

Feeling the turmoil she was suffering, I wanted to comfort her. The thought of her pain tugged at my heart. Seeing her sadness so visible, I made a promise that would become sacred to me, "I promise you something, Ruth. Sometime in the future, I will see and talk to your son when he returns from Afghanistan."

"What? Why would you do that?" She asked, not sure of my intentions.

"I want to remind him of what a good mother you were to him. I will tell him things you wanted him to know, how much you loved him growing up and how much you still love him. When I finish, he will never forget you, for you never forgot him."

She asked again, somewhat in disbelief, "Why would you do this for me?"

"I want to do it because in the Bible you read to your son what Jesus said: *Love one another as I have loved you.* With that sense of love in me, after I talk to your son, he will always cherish the memories he has of you and never forget the feelings you have for him."

Hope filled her face, replacing the anguish that was there a few minutes ago. As her eyes focused on me, they stared at something more than skin deep. She said, "You truly are what others here have said you were. You're someone who knows the Lord."

"I try to be the person God wants me to be."

Ruth persisted, "YOU ARE the person God wants you to be. Before this illness, I'd never spoken to anyone about life and death, let alone my thoughts about God. Don't get me wrong. I've always believed in the Lord. I've just kept my feelings to myself. But there's something about you, Naomi. I feel comfortable talking to you."

"You can talk to me about anything, especially whatever troubles you."

"I do want to talk to you about something that concerns me." Fear suddenly became visible in Ruth's face as she admitted, "More than anything else, I'm afraid of death."

"Let me tell you what I believe will happen."

"Please tell me," she pleaded, eager to know more.

"Some say when one finally closes their eyes in death it is a blessing in that one passes from this world into one where there is no more pain or sorrow. Helen Keller, the famous blind author, once said it is no more than passing from one room into another. But, she went on to explain there would be a significant difference for her. In that other room, she would be able to see. For God would be there to take her by the hand on her journey into Heaven."

"Oh, I do hope you're right."

"If I am right, God will make it possible for your eyes to see the universe and Heaven itself as no mortal could ever imagine it."

"Then perhaps I will be able to see my loved ones that have gone on before me."

"It's long been my thinking, the person or persons who have loved you the most in this life will visit you when your time comes. Perhaps, only you will be able to see them, in your mind's eye, or in dreams or visions."

"I know I'm going to die soon," Ruth reflected, thinking about it. "When I was young, death was something so far off I didn't think of it. If I had properly considered it, I would've lived my life quite differently. Please tell me what you think. Is it too late for me?"

"It's never too late. The Lord is always waiting for you to accept Him. He's waiting, with His arms stretched out to encircle you with His love."

"I wish I understood the Lord a little better."

"The Lord is all around us. His spirit is everywhere. He is the Good Shepherd. We are His sheep. Sometimes some of those sheep become lost. He searches for those lost, bringing them back into the fold. I know He does because I was one of those lost sheep."

Ruth had been taking in my every word and asked, "How does one know if one has become lost?"

"Probe deeply into your own heart and soul. Clearly examine yourself. Then you will know."

"Naomi, will you pray for me?"

"I will, right now." Holding her hand, phrases from the 23rd psalm streamed through my mind. I prayed aloud, "Lord, we are here, your two servants–Ruth and Naomi–who wish to pray. You, Lord, are our shepherd. As we make our way through this life, please lead us in the paths of righteousness for Your name's sake. Restore our souls even as we walk through the valley of the shadow of death. We will fear no evil, for You are with us. May Your goodness and mercy be in our hearts all the rest of our days. And at the end of our lives, may we dwell in Your house, the house of the Lord, forever and ever."

Finished, I looked down into Ruth's eyes, which were full of the feelings she felt. "I love you," she whispered. "The Lord sent you to me. You're a healer of souls, helping those that need help. As you were praying, I felt my soul open up, and the Lord filled it with His spirit. Now, when He decides to take me, I'm no longer afraid to die."

Leaning closer, I kissed her on the cheek. Reacting, Ruth reached up with her fingers, delicately touching the features of my face. She whispered, "You are among the most truly good persons I have ever had the honor to know. Please come back before the day's over with."

"I will, I promise I will," I emphasized that I would as I prepared to leave for a full day ahead of me. During the next several hours, I would meet with others in desperate stages of need. By the end of the day, I realized how much I was serving a purpose here. The Lord's spirit was working through me, helping those who needed to find peace.

Thoughts of Ruth had lingered in the back of my mind, never leaving me. I didn't feel like I was done until I saw her again.

Reaching room 203, I stood in her opened doorway, only to be greeted by her smiling face. Sitting up in her raised bed, she said, "I knew you would come back. Please come in. I have something for you."

Entering, I felt something positive, a new element that was not in her room earlier. Sitting down in the chair beside her bed again, I asked, "What is it, Ruth?"

She pointed to the overbed table on the other side of her hospital bed that had been pushed away. Being one of those custom tables attached to a four-wheeled base that slides beneath the bed, Ruth explained, "I was using it earlier. After you left this morning, I had the nurse roll it over here and bring me pen and paper. I wrote my son a four-page letter, telling him about you bringing faith back into my life and that because of you, I'm not afraid to die now. I let him know that he should come and visit you here when he gets back from Afghanistan. Hopefully, he won't miss me so much after he reads my letter."

"You're one of a kind, Ruth. Of course, he's going to miss you. There's not another mother quite like you."

"Naomi, you've been so good to me today. I hate to, but I have one more favor to ask of you."

"Anything, I'll do anything for you."

"I just finished the letter, not 30 minutes ago. I made out the envelope, and it's ready to be mailed. Would you see it gets to the post office for me?"

"I'll make sure of it, I promise."

"After going to the other side of her bed to retrieve it, I turned to see something in her room I hadn't seen before.

Across the room, a framed picture had been hung on the opposite wall. It depicted Jesus holding a single sheep just like in the story I had told Ruth earlier. Staring at it in amazement, I said, "That picture, it wasn't here earlier."

"Whenever I look over at that wall," she said, telling me her thoughts, "I see the good shepherd holding his lost sheep."

I asked, "Where did it come from?"

Ruth explained, "It showed up shortly after you left this morning. Isn't it amazing how the eyes of Jesus seem to be staring directly at me as if He is watching over me?

"Yes," I agreed, "it's as if the spirit of the Lord is right here in your room."

"Since this morning, I've been praying and thinking of Jesus a lot. But, then, it was kind of strange. A woman I'd never seen before came in and hung this picture on the wall over there. I mentioned I'd never seen her before, and she said she'd been at *All Souls* since the doors opened. Oh yes, she said you were a good friend and that you would understand. I believe she said her name was Sister Mary."

"Oh yes," I whispered, "Sister Mary, of course."

"Just talking with her, she seemed a lot like you, close to God. But yet, she seemed a little different than anyone I'd ever met." Pausing for a moment, thinking about it, she added, "You know, it was almost like she was some sort of angel."

"Sister Mary has had that effect on others here at *All*

*Souls*," I said, agreeing but not revealing the whole truth of what I knew.

Moving closer to Ruth, I took her hand into mine, elaborating on my feelings, "I really do think the presence of Jesus is in this room and will watch over you for the rest of your time here."

"You know what I'm thinking," said Ruth, looking up at me. "I've often wondered why I didn't die six months ago like the doctors said I would. Now I know for sure."

"Why is that?"

"God wanted me to meet you."

Embracing Ruth, I could feel spiritual energy in the room. Ours was a special friendship that was meant to be. The memory of just knowing her will be treasured within my heart forever.

As I left Ruth's room, I glanced over at the painting once more. Perhaps it was the way a ray of light came through the blinds, casting a golden aura around the face of Jesus, for it seemed to escape the canvas and travel across the room. Its healing warmth seemed to surround Ruth as she rested. This sight lingered with me as I went back downstairs.

An inner need filled me as I entered my room after a long day. Kneeling by my bedside, I prayed for Ruth, "Lord, please be with her. She's a good person, worthy of You."

"God knows this," said a familiar voice coming from behind me. Looking around, I saw the figure of Sister Mary standing by the window.

Getting to my feet, I went over and told her what I knew in my heart, "The presence of Jesus from your painting should help her a lot."

"You're right. In her sleep, she will dream of Jesus and have visions of Him. He will comfort her and set her at peace. You see, my child, God does work in mysterious ways."

I had to admit again, "Just when I think I understand God, something happens that makes me realize there's so much I don't know. There are so many things to learn."

"Mankind has only barely scratched the surface of the full meaning of God's words. It's too much for the human mind to fully grasp. That is why God IS God, and we are but mere mortals."

Taking in the full weight of her every word, I repeated my desire in all sincerity, "There is so very much I want to learn, to know and understand our Lord."

"Naomi, in time, you will come to know the full meaning of God. Remember what Jesus said, *Seek knowledge, and you shall find it. In time, wisdom will be given unto you.*"

Going to bed that night, I prayed for the wisdom Sister Mary talked about. In the days to come, I would need that wisdom in giving hope to those who needed it.

# CHAPTER 12

# Meeting Timmy Jones

I arrived at *All Souls* in late February, and now it was late March, having been here almost a month. Getting up early one morning, I looked over to see Sister Mary standing across the room by the dresser there. Gesturing at a jewelry box sitting on it, she said, "I want to give you something."

"Something for me?" I asked, wondering what Sister Mary wanted to give to me. Going over beside her, I asked, "What is it?"

"Naomi, this used to be my jewelry box. Open the bottom drawer."

As I slid it open, I could see a beautiful cross attached to a chain, occupying the whole drawer.

"It's stunning," I said, admiring it.

"It was mine for many years. Wearing it made me feel closer to the Lord. It will do the same for you. I want you to have it."

"But it's yours," I protested.

"It's not doing me any good gathering dust inside this jewelry box. My child, please, wear it for me."

Picking the cross up, I could feel Sister Mary's love within it. "I'm honored. In wearing it, I will always feel your love near me."

"Bless you, Naomi, for it is I who is honored to have you wear it."

"When I'm not wearing it," I explained, "it will never be far from me. Somehow, I already know, with it nearby, I will feel His love and presence for every moment of the rest of my life."

"By you wearing this cross, in a world falling apart, full of hate and violence, it will let others know the Prince of Peace is also here. You see, one day in a fast-coming future, He will work His miracle of peace and love within the hearts and souls of all mankind."

"I pray that day will come, perhaps in my lifetime."

"My child, keep praying for that to happen, and one day it will. Our Lord promises that one day He will return and make the world anew, into a shining beacon of hope that will glimmer throughout the Universe."

Sister Mary's words echoed in my head while getting dressed for a new working day. I whispered, "Lord, our world needs your Holy Spirit within all of us, now more than ever."

Later, walking the second-floor halls with Chaplain

Andrews, he looked over at me, recognizing something familiar around my neck, "That's Sister Mary's cross you're wearing."

"I know. She gave it to me earlier this morning."

Stephen remembered, "She used to say it comforted our patients to see her wear it. It was especially so with the younger ones. Unfortunately, the young children we see here are terminal cases. You know, it doesn't surprise me she gave it to you. I think it will help you, especially today."

"Why do you say that?"

"Because today you're going to be meeting a young boy who puts a lot of faith in the cross of Jesus." Stopping for a moment, he studied me closely. "I know you're good with adults, but do you think you're strong enough to work with little children who are terminal cases? What do you think?"

"No matter what our ages are, we are all God's children. My relationship with Him is becoming stronger every day. As I walk with Him and talk with Him daily, He guides me in what to say and do."

"I'm glad to hear you say that, for it will take every ounce of your strength in dealing with the small children we have here. It will take all the love and understanding you have to give."

I sought to put his mind at ease. "I will give my all to the little ones within *All Souls*. I have embraced the words of Jesus, *It is more blessed to give than to receive*. From these words, I mean to give all my heart to the little children here."

"When we see Timmy Jones today, be prepared to do what you've just said. I know you will. He's a very special little boy who's in the last stage of his life."

"Jesus told me what to do when He said, *Suffer the little children not, and forbid them not to come unto me, for of such is the kingdom of Heaven.*"

"Bless you, Naomi, Jesus is with you."

As we resumed walking down the hall to Timmy's room, a thought started forming in my head: Within a hospice, sometimes love between the patient and caregiver can become the purest, most powerful form of love one will ever experience. It can touch your soul. This was about to happen to me.

Entering the little boy's room, Stephen introduced me, "Good morning, Timmy. This is the lady I've been telling you about. This is Miss Naomi, my new assistant. She'll be seeing you on a regular basis."

The little boy looked up at me with bright, loving eyes. He asked, "May I call you Miss Naomi?"

"You may call me 'Miss Naomi' or just 'Naomi,' whichever pleases you."

"Good, may I also call you my friend?"

"I'd be very glad if you did." I took his hand in mine, comforting him as I continued, "Somehow, Timmy, I think I'm always going to be your friend."

I felt compassion and love for him. Even though the Lord brings so many of us together without us humans realizing it, I distinctly felt the invisible hand of God bringing little Timmy and me together.

The sight of this young boy's pale, emaciated body was truly heart-rendering. As I prepared to leave, his little arms and hands clung to me, begging for my love. I knew that in the days to come, I would give it unsparingly, with all my heart.

Back out in the hall, beyond earshot of Timmy's room, I asked, "What's wrong with Timmy?"

A grave expression formed on Stephen's face as he whispered, "His body is ravaged with stage four, terminal cancer."

The words just came out of me, "He needs me."

Stephen looked at me knowingly, "I told you so. Timmy's little soul will take all the love you can give."

"I will give him all that I have and then some. I can't wait to see him again." I had already made up my mind to see him first thing the next morning. Some people go through their whole lives and never express the love they feel for someone. This little boy reached out to me with his love within minutes after meeting me. It set me to thinking. I don't want to get to the end of my life and realize that I let something so wonderful slip through my fingers. Love can be a fleeting thing if we don't grab hold of it before we lose it. With this little boy, I felt a mother's love from the very beginning.

Bright and early the next morning I stood in the doorway of the boy's room. I said, "Good morning, Timmy," in a tone of voice that he instantly knew I wanted to be there.

Looking up, a smile spread across his face in immediate recognition. "Miss Naomi!" Excitedly, he extended his arms toward me, beckoning me forward into his room. Sitting down in the chair by his bed, his eyes never left me as he added, "I knew you were coming this morning. God told me you would."

I had found something extraordinary in this little boy. A loving spirit was alive within him. But there was also a huge sense of aloneness inside him as well. He opened up about it immediately, "I'm just a small person who doesn't have anyone."

Big tears formed in his eyes as I asked, "But, how is that so?"

Leaning forward, Timmy buried his face in his hands, trying to wipe those tears away. Swallowing hard, he looked back up at me, speaking a little above a whisper, "I'm sorry, Miss Naomi, it's hard for me to talk about it. I'm told my mother passed away when I was born. My daddy raised me till he got sick and died a couple of years ago. That was just when I first started getting sick too. There was no one else in my family. I'm all alone now...."

As he went silent for a moment, I felt a mother's love fill my heart again. Taking his shaking hand, my own feelings found words, "You're wrong, Timmy. You're not alone. You have me and someone greater than me, Almighty God."

Trying to smile, the tears near the edges of his eyes began to stream down his face. Staring up at me, he said,

"I don't know how to explain it. Everything inside me hurts except when I'm near you. Then I feel better."

"The Lord wants you to feel better. That's why I'm with you right now."

"Oh, Miss Naomi, I love you so much." His eyes cleared, and almost instantly, all signs of pain left him.

Giving him my support and love in return, I let him know, "I'll be right here, as long as you need me."

Timmy's eyes filled with love as his words revealed what he was thinking, "I wish you could be my mommy."

I answered what was in my own heart, "I know that while you are here, I'd like to be your mommy."

Timmy squeezed my hand affectionately, replying, "I'd like that with all my heart."

"It's done then. For the rest of your life, I'll be your mother, and you will be my son."

We embraced each other, knowing this was what God wanted. I thought in my heart, this is right. For a time, I believe I found a mother's love for this little orphan boy. As I look back on it now, I see something very clearly. In the grand scheme of our lives, those of us that find and experience true love are truly the lucky ones.

After I left Timmy's room, even though I saw many other patients that day, my mind was full of thoughts of this little boy. Early the next morning, I went straight away to his room. I had to see him. His cheerful face greeted me again.

With equal warmth, I whispered, "My boy, Timmy."

Immediately, a question popped out of his little mouth, "Miss Naomi, what brought you to *All Souls*?"

"God brought me here so I could meet you."

"But how is it that you know the Lord?"

"I met Jesus in a vision right here in our own chapel down on the first floor. Approaching the altar, I saw Him on the cross, and He spoke to my mind."

"What did He say?"

"He forgave me of my sins and asked me to serve Him, right here within these walls. That's how I came to be here."

After telling him of my own experience, I felt the special bond between us growing stronger. Timmy had listened intently, and now his heart's desire came to the surface, "Oh Miss Naomi, I want to know Jesus as you know Him. I've never been to our chapel. Would it be possible? Please, if you take me, I know I'll have the strength. Please!"

I could see the sense of urgency in his face as he begged me. In my heart I knew this would be the right thing. So, I made arrangements with Stephen to make this happen.

Securing Timmy in a wheelchair with a safety belt, I took him downstairs. Pushing the wheelchair from the elevator, we went down the long hall to the chapel. Inside, we went slowly down the center aisle toward the altar.

Seeing the awe and wonder forming on his face, I understood what he was feeling. It had been the same with me back on that fateful day in late February. The presence of the Lord was still there, a few feet in front of us at the altar.

Timmy looked up at me, asking, "Could you unfasten the safety belt? I promise I'll be okay. I have the strength. I want to approach the altar on my own."

A voice inside my head told me to do it. Obeying the voice, I unfastened the belt, gently helping him out of the wheelchair and to his feet.

Steadying himself with a newly found strength, which surely had to be from the invisible hand of God, he looked up to reassure me, "I'll be okay, mother. I promise."

It was the first time he called me 'mother,' and it made me feel good. I responded to reassure him, "I'll be right here if you need me."

Observing him, I knew that my help wasn't needed. His strengthend legs carried him the extra few feet to the altar. Seeing the determination in his face made me admire him all the more.

As Timmy prayed, I felt a presence next to me. I turned to see Sister Mary standing near me. "He'll be alright," she said, "Jesus knows this little boy." Before I could say anything, she vanished. From her comment, though, I knew Timmy was already a child of God.

Afterward, as I helped Timmy back in his wheelchair, I noticed his concentration was still on the cross anchored to the altar table. I asked, "What is it, son?"

He looked up at me, smiling knowingly. "I saw Jesus. He touched me."

"Did He say anything?"

"Yes, He said though I wouldn't be able to see Him, He would still be watching over me and be with me always."

Later, after we got back to Timmy's room and he was back in bed, he asked me, "Does the Lord ever speak to you?"

I explained as best I could, "When I'm in a quiet place, and I concentrate hard enough, I can hear His voice from Heaven speak to my soul. He lifts me up and helps me be the person I am to you."

Timmy looked up at me admiringly.

I asked, "What are you thinking?"

"You often seem to be surrounded by a golden light."

"It's God's golden light."

"Just what is that?"

"It's His warmth surrounding me, sustaining me. More than we ever know, sometimes the Lord is with us, inspiring us to do the things we do. He has inspired my awareness of so many things I did not know. Now, I'm caught up in my mission in life, which is to serve Him."

Timmy leaned over and kissed my hand. Looking back up at me with love in his eyes, he said, "Mother, you're a good person."

"Having the spirit of Jesus inside my soul was His greatest gift to me. Now, it's His greatest gift to you."

He smiled. "I feel warm and safe when I'm with you, mother."

"I like it when you call me that."

Seeing the look of love in each other, we gently hugged.

Through the touch of his little hands, I could feel his love for me. It was something I had long since given up the thought of ever genuinely feeling from another human being.

Leaving Timmy's room that afternoon, I whispered to myself, "Thank you, Lord, for allowing me to know this little boy and give him a mother's love." I knew I would love him and pray for him for the rest of his short life.

# CHAPTER 13

# Easter Sunday

Since arriving at *All Souls*, every waking moment had been changing me. Each day I was trying to accomplish something positive. Being in a place that was one step away from Heaven in many ways, a lot was coming together within me on my life's journey.

In this new month, Easter Sunday would be upon us soon. The coming days would be like none that I had ever experienced. Many souls would feel the presence of God more than ever before.

I was on my way to a meeting with Chaplain Andrews when I heard voices from within his office as I drew near. I thought better of just walking in and knocked first on his office door.

"Yes, who is it?" There was an element of surprise in the Chaplain's voice.

"It's me, Naomi," I answered from outside in the hallway. "I'm here for our meeting."

"Oh yes," his voice became hesitant before he continued, "just one moment, now come on in."

As I opened the door, he looked up at me and said, "I've been expecting you." Though he said it, his facial features expressed surprise at seeing me.

As I entered his office, my eyes surveyed the room. There was no one else there but Stephen, sitting behind his desk. Seating myself across from him, I was sure he could see my surprised expression. So, I mentioned it right off, "I heard voices from the hall, but there's no one else here."

"I cannot lie," he said, resigned to telling me the truth." You did hear voices."

I asked, "What is it, Stephen? Over the past month, I've gotten to know you. I feel like I know the soul of the man sitting across from me. I also know the secret of *All Souls* as well, that it's still inhabited by the spirit of its founder."

"You're right. You do know me." He relaxed as he revealed, "Sister Mary was here a few moments ago, sitting in the very seat you're occupying now. She was just suddenly there, wanting to talk to me. It was important, and I listened."

"If I may ask, what did she have to say?"

"She wants us to have a service, made up entirely of gospel hymns on Easter Sunday."

"Right here in our own chapel?"

"Yes, she thinks it would uplift the spirits of all our

patients who could attend. It would mean having our nurses and nurse's aides here to help transport the patients from their rooms to the chapel. I've wanted to have such a service for a long time, but I guess I've had lingering self-doubts about the practicability of doing it."

"I think it's an inspired idea!" I broke in with enthusiasm. "Through Sister Mary, it's the Lord telling us to do it."

Stephen sat there for a few moments, thinking this through. Then, his face lit up with an expression of acceptance. "Yes, we're going to do it! An Easter service of Christian hymns would strengthen the souls of everyone in attendance."

I agreed in an even broader way, "It will strengthen the faith of everyone within these walls."

Leaning forward across his desk, Stephen gently touched my hand. "Your enthusiasm is exactly what I needed to hear. All around us, in this modern world, many have forgotten who the Lord is. We need more faith in our lives. We need to be courageous and stronger in a Godless world where many have turned their backs on Him. After all, it was He who shed His blood for our sake."

"Stephen, I'm so grateful God brought me here. I believe He brought us both here for a purpose, His purpose."

As I left his office, both our hearts were uplifted. Standing in the hallway for a moment, I felt so near to God. I could hear Jesus whispering to my mind, *I am with you always.* I asked myself, could I do no less for Him?

Going upstairs, I went to see Timmy Jones straight away. Standing in the doorway to his room, I saw his little face look up at me. For a brief instant, a touch of sadness went straight through me to my heart. Knowing this would probably be Timmy's last Easter was a thought almost too much for me.

Sitting down in the chair by his bed, I got on eye level with him. Taking his little hand, wanting to get as close to him as possible, I tried to smile as I said, "Good morning, my little boy."

Even though he was very ill, his eyes were still incredibly sharp, seeing through my attempt at cheerfulness. "Why were you so sad just then when you stood in the doorway?"

"I wasn't sad," I said, trying to brush it off.

Ignoring my denial, he told me, "You were thinking my time is short, but I don't want you to think about that."

"I can't help it. I love you so much."

"You made something possible when you took me to the chapel the other day."

"What did I make possible?"

"I spoke to Jesus at the altar table. He was in my room last night, sitting in the very chair you're sitting in now. He's been coming to see me often, watching over me."

"Timmy, did He say why He was in your room?"

"He didn't want me to be afraid anymore. He was here to protect me. That made me feel good. I'm not afraid of anything now."

A familiar voice from the opened door spoke up, "That's right, Timmy, Jesus can make all of us feel good."

I looked over to see Chaplain Andrews standing in the doorway. Entering the room, he came along the other side of Timmy's bed. As he got closer, the little boy's excitement became visible.

"Wow, Chaplain Andrews, it's mighty good to see you!"

"You're a pretty important little boy."

"I am?" Timmy asked as a smile formed on his face.

"In fact, I wanted to see you about something really special we have planned."

"What's that?"

"Easter Sunday is coming up. Our whole service, in the chapel on the first floor, is going to consist of Christian songs. I would like you to be our guest of honor and sit in the first row, right in front of the altar." Looking over at me, he added, "Naomi can bring you down in your wheelchair, that is if you'll come."

With the look of excitement still on his face, Timmy answered, "I sure will! Thank you, Chaplain!"

Making sure, Stephen asked, "Then, it's settled?"

"May I ask a few things?" Several questions seemed to come to the little boy all at once.

"Sure, Timmy, what is it you want to know?"

The little boy was very serious, asking, "May I sing along too? Would it be okay?"

"Of course, you can. In this service, everyone can sing

along."

"I like that." Looking satisfied, Timmy added, "I've always wanted to sing at a church service. It's something I've never been able to do in my whole life."

"Well, you'll get that chance this Sunday."

Almost as an afterthought, the little boy asked, "Will there be songs about Jesus? You see, Jesus is very important to me."

Stephen explained, "Our entire service will be to glorify the Lord. I believe the spirit of Jesus will be there Easter Sunday, and you will connect with Him."

"Oh Chaplain, I know I will." A look of awe and wonder filled Timmy's face. It was though strength was returning to the little boy's body, just enough so he could go to the chapel.

After Stephen had left, I bent over and kissed Timmy's forehead as I prepared to continue my rounds. Looking up at me, he said, "I love you, Naomi, so very much."

Feelings straight from my heart formed the returning words, "I love you too, my son."

Reaching up with his little hand, his fingers touched me, getting my attention. "One thing more," he said, "sometime after Easter Sunday, I'm going home to the Lord. It'll be the happiest day of my life when I'll be able to walk from this room, hand in hand with Jesus."

After I left Timmy's room, I soon realized the word was spreading all over the second floor about our Easter Sunday service. Upon entering Ruth Wilson's room, she looked at me and asked, "What's this I hear about a Sunday service in the chapel?"

Before I could answer, the nurse who was attending to Ruth, slightly elevating her bed, also inquired, "Is the Chaplain going to conduct a service comprised completely of songs?"

"He most definitely is," I answered. "The Chaplain feels it will not only help but inspire all of those within *All Souls* who can attend."

An internal light seemed to come on and lighten Ruth's face. Looking directly at me, almost pleading, "Would it be possible for me to attend? Just as you spoke of it, I felt something inside myself telling me it would be good for me."

I glanced over at the nurse, Ann Bishop, who was still in the room. She'd been here for several years, so I sought her opinion. "Nurse Ann, what do you think? Would it be possible for Ruth here to come to the chapel on Sunday?"

"I'll have to weigh that." Nurse Ann looked over at Ruth, silently evaluating her condition. I could almost see the wheels turning inside her head as she was a thoughtful person who came from something of a religious background herself. Focusing on me now, she answered, "A service of gospel music has been known to produce a certain amount of spiritual energy that has the potential to strengthen all those in attendance. Some say they feel God's presence in such a service. Yes, if Ms. Ruth here is as strong as she is now, she might be up for it Sunday."

Ruth reacted positively to that assessment, "I will be strong enough, I know in my heart, the Lord wants me to go."

"I feel it too," I added. "Bless you, Ruth. His hand will be with you, strengthening you Sunday."

Later on, as I left Ruth's room, Nurse Ann, who had lingered on with us, followed me out in the hall. Calling after me, she asked, "May I talk to you for a bit, alone?"

"Sure, where can we go?" I could see something was on her mind, something she needed to talk about.

She suggested, "We could go upstairs to the family room. There's no one there this time of the morning."

Taking the elevator to the third floor, it opened almost directly into the family room. This was where relatives and friends of patients sometimes gathered. At one end were large glass doors that opened up to a rooftop patio. There was an excellent view of the skyline and the stars above at night.

I remarked, "I've never been up here before or to the lunchroom across the hall. Someone's always brought me a sandwich or something. I guess I've been too absorbed in my work."

"It can be a whole different world up here sometimes," Ann revealed.

Looking around, I noticed a portable telescope sitting over in the corner. "What's that for?"

"That belongs to Chaplain Andrews," Ann explained.

"Astronomy is his hobby. Sometimes he comes up here at night just to look at the stars or just think and clear his head." Pausing, focusing on me, she added, "That's what I want to do, clear my head."

"Ann, can I help you in some way?"

"Yes, you can. Having not been here very long, you don't really know me. We haven't had much of a chance to talk. But I have noticed you. You're so good with the patients. I've seen how so many are uplifted after talking to you. I thought maybe, since you're a person of faith that you possibly could help me."

Seeing that she was reaching out to me, I took her hand, reassuring her, "Sure Ann, what is it?"

"I want to come to the service Sunday. I want to help you with the patients, any way I can."

"Of course, you can, but you didn't need to ask me about that." I could tell something else was troubling her. "There's something else. It's okay. You can open up with me."

A look of relief came over her face. "Everyone says you're easy to talk to, now I know. It may seem silly to you, but I grew up on a small farm out from Holdenville, where we kids kept to ourselves. Back then, before I went to nursing school, I didn't communicate with others very well. It was only when I went to a small country church did I really begin to open up, singing gospel songs there."

"Perhaps that's what God wanted you to do."

"At the time I thought that too, that I would grow up to

become a gospel singer. But as I grew older, I got away from the church and went to nursing school. For several years I've thought my true calling was to be a nurse. Lately, though, I've been thinking that I should have pursued my original child-hood dream. On the other hand, over the years, I believe I've become a good nurse. Naomi, what do you think I should do?"

"If you feel strongly about something, you should act upon it. You just might feel the Lord's hand reaching out to help you accomplish it. Perhaps He wants you to sing again, as well as being a nurse."

Ann digested that thought for a moment, then asked, "Do you really think that might be possible?"

"Sure, it's possible. Sometimes we never know where the roads of life are going to take us."

"But where do I begin?"

"Ann, I have an idea. Why don't you sing Sunday? I'll introduce you, and you sing something you know from your childhood."

"Yes, I could do that. Thinking about it, I would sing something my old great grandmother taught my mother as a child. Back in 1878, my great grandmother attended a church in Dallas where she heard a song written and sung by a singing evangelist, Knowles Shaw. He died tragically right after that, but the song stayed with her for the rest of her life. It's stayed with me too. I haven't sung publicly since my par-ents died, but if I could, I'd like to sing that song, Sunday."

"Of course, you can. I think it was the Lord's purpose we talked about this. Ann, I hope we can be friends from now on out."

She squeezed my hand and said, "The best of friends."

That evening, returning to my room, I saw Chaplain Andrews in the hallway. I let him know my impression, "Everyone's excited about Easter Sunday."

He agreed, "I saw that too. Ann Bishop came by. She said you talked to her. I've been trying to get her to sing for years. She has a wonderful, soulful voice, yet nothing I could say would convince her to sing. Yet you said something that changed her mind."

"All I said was I thought God wanted her to sing."

"That may be, but there must have been something in the way you said it. I've noticed there's always passion in your voice when you talk to people. You have the gift of being able to reach others in their hearts."

"Stephen, I think with all that's happening, the Lord has a purpose on Easter Sunday. I feel His hand at work to restore some measure of faith that has been lost in all of us."

He looked at me thoughtfully. "I think you could be right."

"In more ways than we could possibly know, I believe the Lord is healing us from within. He's restoring our souls."

The next morning, I had positive thoughts fill my head. I wanted to visit with Ruth first thing. Something fresh and good was about to happen in all our lives. I felt it from the moment I stepped out of the elevator onto the second floor.

Heading toward Ruth's room, I could hear multiple voices coming from there, even before I got to the door. As I reached the doorway, there before me was Nurse Ann with Timmy in his wheelchair. They were visiting with Ruth, who was sitting up in bed. The atmosphere was positive and upbeat, like the hand of the Lord was strengthening them. During the day, I found this to be so with everyone on the second floor. I knew in my heart, God's love was penetrating everyone's mind, working a miracle.

Ruth's face lit up. Her smiling expression connected with me as she elaborated, "Oh Naomi, we're all so excited about tomorrow. I've been visiting with Timmy and Ann here. It's sort of strange, I didn't expect it, but I'm feeling a sense of belonging coming back into my life this morning. Timmy's such a wonderful little boy. He reminds me of my son at that age."

Timmy spoke up, "I was telling Ruth here, I would only go if she would get out of that bed and go to the chapel with me Sunday."

Watching Timmy and Ruth, I could see a sense of joy and renewed hope reflected in both their faces. As they continued to talk, Nurse Ann quietly came over by me and whispered, "I'm seeing that we have a golden opportunity to do something that will be good for everyone within these walls."

Agreeing, I whispered back, "You're right, but there's something else going on here."

"What else?"

"Ann, I'm seeing God's involvement in all our lives, making us better persons as well."

Ann looked over at Timmy talking to Ruth and seeing how happy they were together. Taking to heart what I said, I could see her becoming moved. She leaned in close to me and said, "I see it too, now. We can all become better persons. What we're doing, it's one more step in the right direction for all of us."

Ann was right. Easter Sunday would be a step in the right direction, lifting up the hearts and souls of everyone.

Sunday morning, as I entered the chapel, there were already a few patients seated. Even though some form of death's shadow was already beginning to appear on most of their faces, so was something else. They all had the appearance of being at peace with God. I wanted to love them all and share the peace they would soon know from our Creator. The spirit of the Lord was uplifting everyone.

Very slowly, with Timmy in his wheelchair and me behind him, I rolled him down the center aisle toward the front row. Getting closer, we made our way to where Timmy wanted to be, directly in front of the altar table.

We were followed by Ann Bishop, behind Ruth in her wheelchair, following us to the front row. Ann saw to it that Ruth's wheelchair was moved close to Timmy so that they could be next to each other. This was something both had wanted, so they could support each other throughout the service.

Being close to both of them, the three of us shared an experience in our minds just then. Perhaps it was an illusion, but perhaps not. It was as though we could hear the hymn of *Nearer, My God to Thee*. Some say this was played by the band on the *Titanic* as it sank.

In his mind, Timmy could hear the words too. "Oh Naomi," he said to me, "I can hear the words, *Angels beckon me nearer. Nearer, my God to Thee.*"

I asked, "Timmy, how do you know those words?"

"I'm not sure, but I think Jesus told them to me in a dream."

As I finished positioning Timmy's wheelchair, I looked over at Ruth. I could see she was delighted to be here. Her expression was full of awe as her eyes took in the whole chapel. She spoke out loud of her impression, "It's beautiful. It so feels like a holy place."

Hearing Ruth as he came up beside me, Chaplain Andrews added, "It is that. I can't explain it. For me, this chapel is more holy than any chapel that has ever existed."

Listening to what they were saying, Timmy echoed them with his own thoughts, "For me, the most holy thing here is this cross, right here in front of us." He nodded toward the gleaming cross, mounted to the altar table.

"That's right, Timmy," agreed Chaplain Andrews. Sitting down in the seat on the other side of the little boy, he got on eye level with him, explaining, "This cross here represents a far different one, an old rugged cross on a hill far away, on which Jesus suffered and died. He stained that old cross with His blood so that a world of lost souls might be pardoned and forgiven of their sins."

"But Chaplain," Timmy's eyes became saddened as he asked, "why did Jesus do that?"

"He did it because of His love for all of mankind. Greater love hath no man more than what Jesus did. His love for us has changed the world and will continue to do so forever. This is why we should cling to the memory of that old rugged cross and ever be true to it."

"I understand," said Timmy, as he reached over and hugged Chaplain Andrews. With a wisdom beyond his years, the little boy had absorbed the full meaning of the chaplain's words.

Standing up, Chaplain Andrews turned to face a small crowd that filled many seats in the chapel. More than two dozen patients, some of their family relatives, and about eight other nurses and hospice workers were here. He began by announcing to this gathering, "On this Easter Sunday, may God shine His light upon us as we sing Christian hymns. Whether any of you realize it or not, the spirit of the Lord is here with us right now. Jesus promised us in the book of Matthew, *Wherever two or more come together in my name, there will I be also.* I believe our faith will become stronger than ever this day. To begin our service, we have our very own nurse, Ann Bishop, with a story to tell about a very powerful song which she will sing."

Chaplain Andrews gestured over at Nurse Ann, who was standing by a nearby piano. All eyes of those gathered focused on her as she told her story, "As a child, I attended a small country church, listening to my mother sing gospel songs. For a long time, I wanted to follow in her footsteps. Hearing her sing this one particular song made me want to sing it. It was written by Knowles Shaw, who was a singing evangelist. He once said it was a great thing to bring people to the cross of Christ through this song. Knowing this, whenever I sing it, real feelings and emotions rise up inside me. So, here it is …" She played the piano as she sang:

> Sowing in the morning, sowing seeds of kindness.
> We will come rejoicing, bringing in the sheaves.
> … sowing for the Master, …
> We shall come rejoicing, bringing in the sheaves.

Though there were more lyrics to *Bringing in the Sheaves*, those are the words I particularly remember. As Ann sang in her haunting, soulful voice, it was every bit as beautiful as she said it would be. I could feel the spirit of the Lord inside her as she sang.

Feeling this spiritual presence within the chapel, it was now my turn to talk about one of my favorite gospel hymns.

"The life of Joseph Scriven was full of tragedy. Upon finding his mother was in poor health, he turned to his faith. Trying to make sense of all the hardship and pain that had befallen him, he put pen to paper, trying to lift his mother's spirits. The Lord inspired him to write what became the hymn I want everyone to sing along with me." Nurse Ann accompanied us on the piano as we sang *What a Friend We Have in Jesus.*

> What a friend we have in Jesus,
> All our sins and griefs to bear!
> What a privilege to carry
> Everything to God in prayer!...

In singing this song, everyone in the chapel felt lifted up by the words that touched all our souls. We continued singing other gospel hymns for almost an hour. A miracle of sorts happened during that time. I watched the faces of those facing death suddenly become reenergized as the words of inspirational hymns escaped their lips.

Nearing the end of the service, Chaplain Andrews spoke of the faith that was strengthening all of us, "I say to all of you, with faith in your hearts, God will help you to overcome whatever life throws at you. When you think you're alone, think about Jesus, and His spirit will be with you. Revelations 19:16 proclaims Jesus to be King of Kings. He is our Royal Master whom we should follow. I have long believed the Lord is my strength and shield. If all of you feel the same as I do, then let us take on the mantle of Christian soldiers. We should embrace what's right in our hearts and let it become our armor in this world. As we look up to the heavens, embrace the hope of salvation to come. Let it become your protective helmet against those that would try to take all hope from you. Become a Christian soldier in the war against a Godless world, one in which mean-spirited souls would try to erase faith in our Lord altogether. Let us declare our faith in song as we sing *Onward Christian Soldiers*."

> Onward Christian soldiers!
> Marching as to war,
> With the cross of Jesus
> Going on before.
> Christ the royal Master,
> Leads against the foe,
> Forward into battle
> See His banners go!
> Onward, Christian soldiers!
> Marching as to war,
> With the cross of Jesus,
> Going on before.

As we sang, I noticed the enthusiasm of everyone; their emotions deeply etched across their faces. Inspiration filled everyone. A new life filled the bodies of those who had been barely alive an hour ago.

I looked over at Chaplain Andrews as the song finished.

The emotions that filled his face were very real. He had put his whole heart and soul into this Easter service.

This same level of feelings was apparent in the faces of everyone present. At the conclusion, Nurse Ann joined me over by Timmy and Ruth. They both were incredibly moved.

Ruth's voice was full of both emotion and feeling, "I can't tell you how much being here has meant to me. Today I actually felt the Lord's presence in this chapel."

Chaplain Andrews revealed his own deep feelings, "God is inviting all of us, in our own little ways, to carry his banner into every nation on the face of this earth."

An excited Timmy spoke up, "It was though the spirit of Jesus was right here, all around us!"

Placing his hand on the little boy's head, Chaplain Andrews whispered, "Timmy, this chapel is a place of miracles. He is here with you, in your mind and heart. The Lord's goodness and mercy will be with you forever."

Being right next to me, the Chaplain also whispered to me, "Naomi, when your work is finished today, please meet me upstairs in the family room. I would like to visit with you."

I answered, "Yes when my work is done, I'll meet you there this evening."

Seconds later, Timmy got my attention once more. Looking up at me, he said in a low voice, "Naomi, mother, I feel something stronger than ever now."

Bending down close to his face, I asked, "What do you

feel, my son?"

"I feel the Lord will be coming for me very soon."

"Why do you say that?"

Before answering me, he glanced over at the cross anchored to the altar table, then back up to me. When our eyes met, he said, "I'll explain when we get back to my room."

As we left the chapel, I looked around into the faces of the patients leaving the service. I saw something. Preparing to roll Timmy's wheelchair back up the center aisle, I saw the same 'something' in Ruth's face. Everyone had the same expression. It was like, without exception, we all had made our own spiritual connections through the gospel hymns sung this day.

Later, in Timmy's room, after getting him back in bed, he looked up at me knowingly, "I suppose you want to know what I was going to tell you when we got back here."

"Yes, very much." Awaiting what he had to say, I sat down in the chair next to his bed.

Reaching toward each other, our hands made a connection. His hand slipped into mine as he told me what happened, "I was sitting in my wheelchair, staring at the cross on the altar table all during the service. I kept feeling the presence of Jesus getting closer to me. Then suddenly, as everyone sang *What a Friend We Have in Jesus*, I could see His face. He told me not to be frightened, that He would be coming for me soon."

"Those were His exact words?"

"Those were the words He spoke to my mind."

"Did He say anything else?"

"Yes, that He would take me through eternity's gate. Even though He told me not to be, I was a little frightened."

"But you're not now?"

"No, because after the service, Chaplain Andrews told me the chapel was a place of miracles. I understood then."

"Timmy, what I'm about to tell you goes beyond the understanding of what many will say, but I know from my own experience it is true. When you say that you have seen Jesus, believe it. What you need now is the hope and love that only He can give you. When you see Him again, remember His loving arms are here to wrap around you and take you the next step of life's journey into all eternity."

"Naomi, I know something I've never told you. I've known it about you for a long time now. Perhaps, it's something you might not even know about yourself."

"What is it? What do you know?"

"Right after we first met, I saw the hand of Jesus touching you, blessing you, Naomi."

I admitted, "I've sensed His presence around me, often, but I've only actually seen Jesus in my visions. Chaplain Andrews is the only other person who knows this about me. No one else knows."

"Your secret is safe with me. I'll be going home with Him, soon enough anyway."

"Timmy, I'm glad you know."

"Mother, I love you with all my heart."

I leaned over and kissed him. "Bless you forever and ever, my little boy, my son."

As I stood up, I noticed him staring at something. "What is it?"

"It's the crucifix you're wearing. It has a glow around it. Somehow, right now, I feel His presence all around you."

"Timmy, when I'm wearing it, I feel connected to our Lord. Something has just started happening to me during the last 24 hours. Even when I'm not wearing it, I still feel His love around me."

"Somehow, I know it. You will have His love around you every day for the rest of your life."

"My son, I think you're right." Just then, a voice spoke to my mind. Immediately, I told Timmy, "I think the Lord wants you to have it tonight." Removing the cross from around my neck, I placed it in his little hand. "Now, Jesus will be with you. You'll be safe and secure with Him tonight."

The little boy reacted, "It feels so warm to the touch."

I explained, "That's because the healing presence of the Lord is within it."

Timmy smiled and did not protest, holding the cross as close to his chest as he could. Somehow, I knew in my heart this little child was going to leave this earth soon. In his final days, he had been growing closer to God, acquiring a sort of sixth sense, actually seeing only what I'd seen in visions and dreams.

As I left his room, I silently prayed for him, loving him with all my heart. Walking out into the hallway, I remembered I had one more appointment to keep before my day would be over with.

.

# CHAPTER 14

# Heaven's Doorway

Exiting the elevator on the 3rd floor, I walked directly into the family room. The lights were off, and it was quite dark by now. Having never been up here at night before, I had no idea that the large picture window afforded such a spectacular view of the heavens. On a clear night such as this, it was easy to see why this window seemed to bring God's creation a little closer to the earthbound spectator.

Not moving, my eyes adjusted to my surrounding in the darkness. I noticed the shadowy figure of Stephen Andrews seated on a sofa over by the picture window. I asked, "What are you doing?"

"Astronomy is my hobby, but I view the stars from a somewhat non-scientific perspective. I'm studying what God has created. Out on our rooftop patio and through this window, I can see a small speck of what is out there."

"As a child," I recalled, "I would gaze at the stars from time to time. Sometimes I thought I could hear God's voice coming from the heavens. The stars are beautiful, but even more so when we realize they are also a work of art and the artist is our Creator."

"Well said, Naomi: You're an extraordinary soul. I just wanted you to know I've been admiring the way you interact with all the patients. By having His spirit within yourself, you've become a witness for Jesus. Patients like Timmy and Ruth have gotten to know Him better through you. I'm sure of it now. You're a wise old soul."

"Stephen, I'm not that old."

"You're old enough to have witnessed the crucifixion of Christ."

"You know my secret. I still wonder, how was it possible that I experienced something that happened 2,000 years ago?"

"I would answer you by asking, how is it possible to look up and see the images of a star reaching Earth, originating from a place where it died thousands of years ago? Considering this, it's not unreasonable for you to be able to see what happened so long ago. God makes all things possible."

I asked, "Is He out there among the stars? Where does God live?"

"Truth be told, God is much closer than out there. His spirit is right here, as you know, within the hearts of all who believe in Him."

"Then what do you look for out there, through your telescope?"

"Letting one's eyes traverse the night sky is where one begins to see no limit to God's power. He is the Creator of all that is out there. Up here at night, I'm in awe of what I see."

"Stephen, what is it that you actually see?"

"I see a Universe full of wonder. There's a lot in the heavens that cannot be explained. These mysteries reveal God in all His glory. If He is out there, I wish that someday I could reach out across space itself, so that I could be in His presence."

"I felt a similar deep need within myself, to get closer to God. All of us will be in His presence one day though when we stand before the throne of God at the end of our lives."

"Again, well said, Naomi. Perhaps God wanted us to visit tonight. I've felt for some time now that the Holy Spirit often guides me in making decisions here. I never felt that more strongly than when I asked you to become my assistant. I'm glad you're here."

"That means a lot to me to hear you say that. Since I came here, I've been feeling like I'm getting closer to the reason I was born into this world."

"Now you've got me curious. What do you think you're here to do in this life?"

"Perhaps it's to be one of those soldiers for Christ we sang about in *Onward Christian Soldiers* today. Or perhaps my ultimate destiny is with God, somewhere out there among the stars."

Stephen seemed to agree, "Perhaps all our destinies will be out there."

I asked, "What would I see, looking through your telescope?"

"You would see that the human race is just a small microscopic bit of God's creation. There is so much more. Billions of other galaxies, millions of light-years away, are scattered throughout the Universe. The mind boggles at what the Creator has done."

Then I remembered, "Sister Mary once told me about all of this."

"Yes, she talked to me also, about all of this, many years ago. With the aid of the Hubble Telescope, astronomers are now saying what she told me so long ago, that the Universe is close to 14 billion years old."

A profound truth filled my mind just then, "Our time on earth is only a blink upon the face of time. But God has been here forever, creating much more than we could ever imagine."

"What do you think that is, Naomi?"

"Beyond what is visible, there is something greater. It just may be Heaven itself."

Thinking about his own childhood, Stephen recalled, "As a young boy, I often gazed at the night sky, imagining what it might hold. I thought for just a little while in my mind's eye, that I too could see Heaven."

"It's amazing," I pointed out, "We can see so much more when God opens up our minds."

Turning on a small table lamp next to the sofa, Stephen's eyes searched my face, recognizing something he saw within me. "I can almost see an understanding of the Creator coming together in you. God's very existence is far beyond man's limited concept of space and time. We must all open up our minds to a new level of thinking when we think of Him."

I understood what he was saying, "Almighty God is the Alpha and the Omega, the beginning and the end of all things. His creation, the Universe, has many parts all woven together in a vast network that the mind of man strains to understand. Yet, He put it together so simply. It is His genius we must all come to know."

Looking up at me, Stephen observed, "Mankind's Creator had a reason and a purpose for us being here."

I thought about it out loud, "From the seed of Adam and Eve, we are God's children. He is our Father in Heaven. We live in a time of extraordinary enlightenment where He is revealing so much to the mind of man."

"In all the years I've studied the heavens," Stephen reflected, "I've learned so much. I see the stars in their courses of an ever-expanding Universe. From the finger of God, since the beginning of time, it stretches from infinity to infinity."

Just then, it was all very clear to me. "What we see out there is but one room of His house. In His home, there are many rooms which are far beyond what the human eye can see."

Listening carefully to my thoughts, he asked, "How is it that you seem to know these things?"

"Many things have not been revealed unto us. Yet every day, it feels like my brain is being filled with knowledge I never possessed before. If human existence continues for a billion years from now, it will only have barely begun to scratch the surface of the wisdom of the Creator. I know this because a voice, one that I recognized as the voice of Jesus, revealed it to my mind."

"What else did He reveal to you?"

"That He is the light of the world. It would be a better place if only those that don't know Him would open the door to their hearts and let His light into their lives."

"Naomi, you speak as if He is right here."

"He is. Though humans cannot see Him, God is very near. His Holy Spirit is all around us, surrounding all humanity, this world, and the entire Universe."

"In all of these places, where do you think Heaven is?" It was his turn to ask the question I had often asked him, but now I had an answer.

"It's where the souls of the faithful will be taken. No mortal knows where that is, but the Bible does say God put a great gulf between us, one that man could never reach. Wherever Heaven's doorway is, Jesus provides us with a pathway. If we follow Him, He will lead us to Heaven."

Stephen remembered, "Jesus did say He was the way, the truth, and the life." Our conversation set his mind to thinking of other possibilities of Heaven's whereabouts. He speculated, "In a strange sense, *All Souls* could be a doorway to where Heaven may be. Through some miracle, Sister Mary's spirit comes from that other reality where Heaven exists. Like an answered prayer, she comes to minister to us as we need help."

I spoke of how she had inspired me, "Sister Mary is like a guardian angel. She has helped bring understanding and hope to others. Through her, I've come to see that the Lord loves all His children. Each time she visits me, she makes His book of life clearer. I see that we are all one step closer in reaching an eternity with God."

Later, on my way back to my room, I kept thinking about Heaven. Feeling the presence of the Holy Spirit around me, explaining, *For each soul beyond this life, one must pass through Heaven's doorway to reach eternity's gate.* In His own way, God will reveal Heaven's doorway to each of us in a time of His choosing. Over the next 24 hours, I would see this very clearly.

## CHAPTER 15

# My Time Has Come

Going to bed that Easter Sunday night, I had an increasing feeling of foreboding take hold of me. Thinking about Timmy, I cried myself to sleep. I couldn't help what was happening, becoming so emotionally attached to this little boy. In such a short time I had come to truly love him as my son.

With Timmy on my mind, I soon slipped into a dream. Perhaps it was more than that. It was so real and life-like. My eyes opened to see him standing by my bed. His little hand touched my shoulder, getting my attention. Focusing on him, I could clearly see he was not in the flesh. Rather he was transparent, sort of a spirit being.

Looking at me with such a caring expression, Timmy whispered, "Miss Naomi, please don't cry for me. I'll soon be all well, walking the streets of Heaven with Jesus."

Sensing another presence nearby, my eyes traveled over to Timmy's other hand. It was being firmly held by a transparent image of Jesus. I heard his voice inside my head, speaking to me, *No longer will this little child suffer. Blessed are all who come unto me as he has, for they will enter my Kingdom.*

The image froze before me, surrounded by a golden aura. Then it quickly dissolved into nothingness. The vision that was there for only seconds was gone.

I lay there in my bed, alone with my thoughts. Becoming fully awake, even though it was still night, I dressed quickly. I knew in my mind and heart I must go see Timmy. I felt like the Lord was calling me to him.

Upon entering the little boy's room, I immediately knew that my fears were well-founded. Though asleep, he was breathing very heavily. It seemed as if his physical body was barely clinging to life.

Going to his side, I could see the strain on his face. I think he could feel the closeness of my presence, for his eyes began to flicker open. As they locked on mine, a steady stream of bright light passed between us. It was the golden light of God surrounding and uplifting both of us.

As Timmy spoke, I could feel the love he had for me. "Miss Naomi, mother, you're here."

"Yes, I had a dream. The Lord wanted me to come to you."

"I was holding on so that I could see you." His trembling hand held up the crucifix I had left with him. "Your cross gave me strength. It comforted me."

"It's the symbol of Christ's triumph over death."

"As I said last night, it felt warm to the touch. After you left, its warmth penetrated my body. I could feel it pass through me, even through my heart and into my soul. It was cleansing the cancer from my spirit, making me ready for my journey."

"Your journey?"

"Yes, I too had a dream last night. The love of God was in this room. A brilliant light appeared in front of my bed. The voice within it said *I am the Lord thy God. Do not be frightened, for I will come for you soon.* I answered, "I will be ready, Lord.""

"Timmy, are you sure?"

"Yes, my body is dying right now. I know my time has come. Looking into that light, I knew I was in the presence of the Creator. Even though I felt His all-consuming love surround me, there was something else, far greater."

"What's that?"

"God's love extends far beyond me. The warmth of His love stretches over the whole world, reaching out to all of God's children. All who open up their hearts to Him can feel His love within themselves. I feel so humbled now."

"Humbled?"

"Being before God was so far beyond anything I could've thought it would be like. He reached into me with a feeling of complete unconditional love. I now have no fear of death because I know that the Creator is real and will always be here for all of us."

Even though Timmy's body was weak, I could see his spirit remained strong because at the core of his soul, he was at peace with God.

Looking up at me, still full of a little boy's curiosity, he said, "Naomi, I know you know. Please tell me what Heaven is like."

"It's a place where time has no meaning. It's a place where you're born again, this time as a spiritual being. All things of the flesh no longer exist. It's a place where there is no worry, no sadness, no pain. It's where you will feel the love and warmth of Almighty God, just as you did last night."

I could see Timmy's eyes searching me as he pleaded, "Please promise me that you'll come and see me when you get to Heaven."

"With all my heart, I promise I will. But you promise me something. When I walk through eternity's gate, you be there to meet me."

The little boy smiled and answered with feelings straight from his heart, "Mother, you can count on it. I'll be there, wanting to hold your hand once more."

"You mean the world to me, my son."

Unspoken emotion filled both of us as he asked something I could not deny, "Would you hold me till I die?"

"Of course, I will." As he had so many times, he touched the deepest regions of my heart.

As I took Timmy in my arms, he handed me the crucifix he had been holding. I placed it on the bedside table next to us, adding, "I'm glad this comforted you last night."

"Mother, it has the power of Jesus in it. After my dream last night, I touched your crucifix, and something else happened. In fact, it's still happening. I still see it."

"What was it?"

"Feeling the presence of something just beyond the foot of my bed, I saw a light, growing brighter by the minute. An image of Jesus was rapidly forming within this light. After a few moments, He emerged from it, coming into this room. I think He wanted me to take His hand and go with Him."

"Timmy, did He leave?" Almost as soon as I asked, I noticed there was a glowing light reflected off the little boy's face.

"Mother, Jesus is still here. He was standing just inside the door when you came in. He's right behind you this very moment. A beautiful light is all around Him. Can't you feel it?"

"Of course. Timmy, I know He's here." My answer was true. Without looking around, I could feel a presence behind me. The light's intensity was penetrating me now. Perhaps it was from something Sister Mary had said, or somehow, I just knew, I could feel the presence of the Holy Spirit in the room.

As I held my little boy, his breathing became noticeably weaker. Yet, he focused on me and whispered, "Mother, the only thing I'm really going to miss is not being with you."

"Don't worry, my son. One day I'll be along, and we will be together, forever in Heaven. For now, though, go with Jesus."

Still looking at me, he answered, "I will." Just then, his eyes were drawn to something beyond me, something I couldn't see. Strength in his voice returning, he said, "I see Jesus in the light, reaching out to me. It's so beautiful. Now I'm sure I know, my time has come."

"My son, go with Him. He will protect you from all harm. Through Him, there is lasting healing. It is forever."

The warmth from the light seemed to penetrate Timmy, reaching inside, transforming him in a way known only to God. His spirit, the essence of his soul was being prepared for its final journey into the light.

I could see the love in his face as he closed his eyes for a final time on this world. As I held him, his breathing relaxed, and he slipped away.

Laying him gently back on his bed, all my feelings for him came to the surface as I whispered softly, "I love you with all my heart, my little son." Standing up, my view took in his whole frail body. My voice cracked as I barely could get the words out, "Go with God." My hand trembled as I slowly made the sign of the cross. It was then I could no longer hold back the tears that streamed from my eyes.

Turning to leave Timmy's room, I look around to see Ann Bishop standing in the doorway. I didn't know how long she'd been there, but she knew I needed comforting as well. As I passed her, she placed her hand on my shoulder and said, "Bless you, Naomi."

Facing Ann, I told her, "Little Timmy's soul has gone into the light with Jesus."

She replied, "That's as it should be. Jesus told us, *I am the light of the world.*" She hesitated for a moment, taking in the grief she saw in my face. I think at that moment, Ann decided to reveal her thoughts, "Something else, I'd like to tell you."

"Yes, what is it?" I was listening.

"The longer you spend at *All Souls,* the more you will come to know that reality is so much more than what we see here. It's also what we feel. Within these walls, you will feel the presence of God many times. It's not so easy for some who come to work here. But Naomi, you're different. I've sensed that from the beginning."

"Ann, I knew the Lord wanted me here from the first day I entered through the doors of *All Souls.*"

We both needed to talk further, so a few minutes later, we were sitting across from each other at a table in the third-floor family room. We were the only two there this early in the morning.

Taking note of that fact, Ann leaned forward, gesturing toward the window, "The sun's just beginning to show itself at the horizon. The morning's about to break on a new day."

Still heartbroken, my words reflected the feelings inside

me, "It'll just be another day of sadness here."

Placing a comforting hand on mine, she said, "We should rejoice that Timmy is not suffering anymore. I saw the brilliant light from the doorway. It's not the first time I've seen it in all my years here. I'm sure you already know this isn't just a hospice. It's what so many others have said, a place of miracles. I believe the Holy Spirit dwells here."

Taking her hand into mine, I said, "I believe that too, with all my heart, for your truth is my truth."

"In my career as a hospice nurse," she continued, "I've worked at other physical, brick and mortar hospices, and you know what I've found?"

"What, Ann?"

"There was a measure of faith in all of them, among both the staff and the patents. With few exceptions, most patients are looking for some kind of closure to their lives."

"You mean like some form of hope to inspire them in their final days?"

"Exactly. Naomi, that's what you seem so good at providing, —getting close to people, giving so much of yourself, even to the point of becoming much more than a friend. You become a kindred soul, going on their final journey with them. That's a rare gift."

"I know everything I do is what God wants me to do."

Ann had a look of recognition form on her face. "Now I know who you remind me of! Many years ago, a very great lady founded and ran *All Souls*. She would say things like, 'she was doing what God wanted her to do! She passed away many years ago. I wish you could've known her."

"But Ann, I did know her. Sister Mary's words continue to guide me to this day. In fact, it was her words that inspired me to enter hospice work."

A questioning expression formed on Ann's face. She looked at me in disbelief. "I don't know how that would've been possible, but this is a place of miracles." Pausing, studying me closely, she added, "You are so much like her. Now, you inspire me to be a better person in my own life."

"Ann, it means so much to have such a good friend as you, here at my side. But giving so much of myself each day, I just wonder, what's next for me?"

She thought about my question for a moment, then gave me the benefit of what she knew, "I can only speak from my own experience. Seeing others going through their final days, discovering faith and redemption, has helped strengthen me. Working with you, I've rediscovered the path which my life should take on this earth. Naomi, you've played so much a part in getting me on that path. I'm truly grateful. As to what's next, only the Lord knows that. But in a place like this, I know it will have a measure of heartbreak."

I feared Ann knew what she was talking about, for an unknown future that would be both trying and surprising lay ahead of me. One thing though, somehow, I knew the future would test me in ways I could only imagine.

# CHAPTER 16

# Heaven Is Revealed

Starting early, with the loss of Timmy still fresh upon my mind, my day would be filled with sadness. The answer to my question, *what comes next?* would soon be answered. Only this time, my sadness would be compounded with more heartbreak.

Not one hour after visiting with Ann Bishop, a voice within me urged me to go see Ruth Wilson. Upon entering her room, I knew immediately she'd been crying. Before I could utter a word, she asked, "Timmy's dead, isn't he?"

I told her what I knew to be true, "He went home with the Lord before sunrise."

"I knew it."

"But how did you know?"

"I had a dream last night in which Timmy came to my room. He told me he would be leaving this world before I woke up. He said he would be there to meet me when I got to Heaven."

I added, "Faith was strong in him. I believe he knew God more than most ever will."

She agreed, "Timmy was a good soul who loved the Lord. I just hope He will forgive me for all the wrongs in my life so I can see that little boy again."

I knew she wanted to be forgiven for what she perceived to be her sins. Sitting down next to her bed, I leaned down and squeezed her hand reassuringly, explaining, "Christ forgave you from the cross. Open up your heart to Him, and when your time comes, He will take you to Heaven."

"Naomi, you always help me to understand that our Lord is a God of love. I found that out after Timmy left. I continued dreaming. Angels came out of a brilliant light above me and spoke to my mind."

I asked, "What did they tell you?"

"They said they were preparing me, that I would be going with them soon, into the light." She paused, staring deep into my eyes. She was searching for some sort of inner truth within me. Then she continued, "They said you would be helping me. So why are you here, really here?"

"I'm here because God wanted me here. His voice spoke to my heart, telling me what to do with my life. He wanted me to help people find their way to Him."

"You've certainly done that. Naomi, you've been good to me. I always thought you were Heaven sent. I just wanted to hear you say it."

"I love you, Ruth."

"Please, tell me more about Heaven."

When she said those words, I somehow knew she would soon be at death's door. Answering her, I spoke the words the Lord put into my heart, "As the door to Heaven opens back, you will be truly humbled by the sight of the Lord in the fullness of all His glory, seated upon His throne. You will barely be able to look at the brilliant light surrounding Him as it is so intense."

It was as though Ruth could actually envision what I was describing to her. She asked, "Where is it? Where is God's dwelling place?"

"Exactly where, is unknown to humankind. But I can tell you it is just beyond the veil of our lives. Soon, you will know and be able to see it."

"Holding her gaze on me, Ruth listened carefully to my every word. She begged, "Please, tell me, what will happen when I die?"

"When you close your eyes for a final time on this life and reopen them again, a miracle will have happened. Jesus will have awakened you to go with Him before the throne of His father, Almighty God, in Heaven. It's a place where the souls of all believers will go beyond eternity's gate. Heaven is more beautiful than the human mind can conceive. The human eye cannot comprehend all the detail and vastness of it."

"Will I ever be able to understand it?"

"All that has been incomprehensible in this life will be understood. Our Lord and savior will make it so."

"On Naomi, how will I get to such a place?"

"Your soul will be taken, as a newborn child, upon angel's wings for your journey into Heaven. As Jesus said, *Heaven is a place of many mansions.* Through Him, you will receive eternal salvation."

Her eyes suddenly became focused on something beyond me, hanging on my every word like never before, beyond what human sight can see. She whispered, "I've lived my whole life for what I see now."

"What do you see?"

"I see Jesus. But something else, you were right about one thing."

"Right about what?"

"Remember, about a week ago, you said I would not die alone, that someone would come to help me crossover."

"Yes, I remember."

"Jesus is not alone."

"Not alone?"

"Little Timmy is with Him, extending his hand toward me."

Though I could not see what Ruth saw, I did feel the presence of the Lord all around us. It made me realize one of the greatest truths: Ultimately, Jesus is our caregiver, the caregiver of all humankind. If we open up our hearts to Him,

He will lift us up and inspire us.

Tears were forming in her eyes as she saw something else. I asked, "What is it, Ruth?"

"I see something in the light above us. I think I see Heaven. It's so beautiful, even more than what you described. Now, something is becoming clearer." Her eyes became awe-struck for a moment as she grew silent. Her eyes strained as she carefully studied what she saw. Still awed by it, she whispered, "It's all golden. It's the holy city of the Lord, the new Jerusalem. I think God wants me to go with Him."

In my own heart and soul, I knew she was right. "It is the Lord coming for you. In a moment, death will be no more for you. He will wipe away your every fear and all of your pain. Death is only a short sleep. Then you will wake up and see our Lord, face to face. He will take you home."

"Naomi, please pray for me."

I looked down at Ruth, feeling so much love for her, and answered, "With all my heart, I'll pray for you."

As I prayed, I saw a soft light form into an aura around her face. It was a spiritual, very holy experience for me. I could feel the presence of the Lord's unconditional love throughout the room. It humbled me to the very core.

She squeezed my hand and said, "I feel such peace now. I can see Jesus clearly now. He's bathed in the golden light above us."

"Ruth, there are so many who want to know about Heaven. You have it within your power to be there in just a short while. You will be able to know our Savior."

"When I stand before God, do you think He will forgive me for not being a better person?"

"You were always a good person. You were a devoted mother who raised a son to be a good man. Don't have any doubt. As human beings, we all have fallen short of the glory of God. The Good Lord knows this. He is a loving and forgiving God. I know in my own heart, He's ready to receive you when you're ready to go."

"Yes, I have to remember our Lord is a loving God. My only regret though is not seeing my son before I go. Remember, I wrote him to come and see you when he returns from Afghanistan. Please help him to understand that I loved him to my dying day. You will, won't you?"

"I promised you I would, and that kind of promise is a sacred promise to me. But I'm going to do more. He's going to hear from my lips that you were a kind and decent person, and in the very end, you went home to the Lord."

Placing her hand in mine again, she smiled. With tears forming in her eyes, she whispered, "I love you for that, Naomi. I feel so much at peace now. I'm just so very tired all of a sudden."

Still holding onto my hand, Ruth drifted off into what would be her final sleep on this earth. Breathing hard, she took one final deep breath. Her hand that clung to me relaxed and became limp. She would soon be gone.

I whispered to her, "Go with the Lord now. May He

uplift your soul and bless you forever and ever."

When Ruth finally let go of this life, I believe she did so in the most peaceful way possible. As it happened, I really believe I could feel God's energy take her soul with Him. After that, what I felt became words, "This is not goodbye, for I will see you again in Heaven."

Ruth's loss pulled at my heart. I could not hold back the tears that rolled down my face. Just as when I lost my mother, this was a blow that would not soon go away. I felt a connection to her that I could not yet explain. She was and is a very special person to me for reasons I will reveal later.

Making the sign of the cross over her lifeless form, I stood up to leave her room. As I turned toward the door, there was Chaplain Andrews, standing in the doorway. Entering the room, he stood motionless right in front of me. After taking in the emotions still quite visibly etched into my face, he commented on something he saw, "You have the reflections of Heaven on your face."

"Maybe that's because Heaven was revealed in what I experienced today. I've had two souls, Ruth just now and Timmy earlier, go home with the Lord today."

Though it was unspoken, I could see he felt for me as he asked, "Naomi, are you okay?"

"I'm deeply saddened. I loved both of them."

"Remember, I told you this hospice would take all you had to give, and then some. You must know your good heart made a difference when it was most needed today."

"I found that because of my love for both of them, I got caught up in their lives, just as if Ruth was my mother and Timmy was my son."

"That's because you're a kind and giving person, qualities that come from your soul. You did the right thing, giving both of them your love and support in their final hours. Perhaps that's your gift. You open up your whole heart and soul to those who need you the most. One thing I know for sure is our world, here at *All Souls*, is a better place with you in it."

I could tell Stephen's words of support came straight from his heart. "I'm most grateful. You make me feel like *All Souls* is my new home."

"It *is* your new home, that is if you want it."

"I want it." I wanted to be here more than any place in my whole life.

As I started to leave, Stephen stopped me with something he was very curious about, "One thing more. Was there anything else you learned from today's experience?"

I didn't have to think twice, answering, "If I hadn't known it already, I now know one thing for sure. Life continues beyond death. With Ruth and Timmy today, I felt the presence of the Lord, ready to take their souls to Heaven."

"You have no doubt?"

"Not in the slightest. I know it to be true."

"What did you see today?"

"I saw a light come out of nowhere from no direct light

source. It formed in both their rooms, above or near them. It was as though the energy that makes up one's consciousness left their bodies, going into this unexplainable light. My faith convinces me, at the time of death, their souls returned to God in Heaven."

"Naomi, I too have witnessed this among dying patients. In some cases, the light was only visible to them. Other times I saw it as well. Over the years, I've talked to many doctors and nurses who have witnessed this happen. They all gave me the same answer that it was unexplainable."

"Just remember Stephen, beyond human medical knowledge, all things are possible unto the Lord. Death is not the end of one's life. For the soul, there is the next chapter in one's existence."

He looked at me, questioning, "What might that be?"

"Beyond death is the light at the end of the tunnel, the light of eternal life."

He stood silent for a moment, absorbing what I had said. "Yes, of course. Naomi, I believe the light is explainable. All of us are children of the light. The Creator is within the light, welcoming the souls of His children into Heaven."

Later, back in my room for the night, I thought about what Chaplain Andrews and I had discussed. Letting things turn over in my mind, I realized the person I was before coming to *All Souls* no longer existed. Back then, I thought and spoke as a child. I did not know the Lord as I do now. God has shown me what I must do with the rest of my life.

This is a very unique occupation I'm in. If you don't have the Spirit of the Lord motivating you, this would not be for you. It will take all the love you can give. Sometimes, events will break your heart. Other times, though, your heart will soar with the greatest satisfaction. In this work, you can become a better person than you ever thought you could be.

As I lay in bed that night, I thought and prayed. We all have precious gifts from Almighty God. My most sincere prayer is that we all begin to use these gifts in His service to transform the world for good.

I prayed for the Lord's guidance in what I should do. In response, I felt His presence within me and heard His words speaking to my soul. And you know something, in a way, it all became a miracle in which He would use me as His vessel to accomplish His will in the days to come.

# CHAPTER 17

# **Decisions**

The next several months led me to help others in their final days on this earth. Totally committed, I put my whole heart and soul into what I was doing.

Walking down the hallways of *All Souls* second floor, you hear all kinds of things: people barely hanging on, screaming out in pain, crying out in fear of death, or just wanting to pray. I believe the Lord was showing me the fragility of human life. Without hesitation, I answered every one of those pleas. As a chaplain's assistant, I ministered to the needs of those souls. This was the mission the Lord had set me upon.

Feeling His presence, I knew God was with me. As each day passed, I grew in compassion and understanding for the sick.

Many have witnessed me uplift the hearts of the dying.

This has led to word of mouth spreading among the patients that I possessed a gift for helping those who needed help getting through the end-of-life experience. In their eyes, I have become God's messenger to them.

As I go from one case to another, I embrace each one of them just the same as I had Timmy and Ruth. Even now, I can still clearly see each one of their faces in my mind. Not a day goes by that I don't think about all of them. I believe with every fiber of my being that the Lord is working through me. Just thinking about it deeply humbles me.

It is now early December, and I hear Chaplain Andrews refer to me more frequently as his assistant with a special gift. It motivates me in ministering to all the sick patients who enter *All Souls*.

Thinking about when Christ walked the earth 2,000 years ago, He did things that only the Son of God could do. Salvation and healing for all people flowed directly from Jesus. Down through history, there have been a few special souls that have acquired some Christ-like qualities within themselves. From Saith Francis of Assisi to Mother Teresa, a few have made their mark for good in this old world.

In a conversation with me in his office, Chaplain Andrews added, "In our own little world at *All Souls*, I would include Sister Mary on such a list of those who have left a positive mark here." Pausing for a moment, he looked at me as if he could see something nobody else could see, then continued, "Something else, through your own actions over the past few months, I'm beginning to believe you have some of those special gifts that will put you on such a list someday."

"Oh Stephen, I'm just one human soul who's trying to follow our Lord's teachings as best as I can."

"By your own humility, you reveal something that is clearly visible to me."

"What could that be?"

"Just as I see it, I believe our Lord's light shines in you."

"You think too much of me."

"Yes, I do, but others have pointed it out to me as well. In your work here, you're doing something beautiful for the Lord. He has given you some of His gifts as you minister to the patients here."

"I admit I let the good Lord guide me in all things, and I will always."

"That was what I wanted to hear you say."

Then I picked up on something in Stephen's voice and his expression. I confronted him, "All of this we've been discussing is not really why you called me to your office, is it?"

Stephen moved a little uncomfortably in the chair behind his desk. "See there; you seem to know what thoughts are in one's mind. It's almost like you possess some form of second sight or ESP."

I confessed, "Sometimes I do feel like I have an inner ability that allows me to pick up what's inside another person's mind. Perhaps it's one of those gifts you think I have. So what is the real reason you wanted to talk to me?"

He explained, "You know I've never really discussed your private life with you, but a matter has come up in the past couple of days that forces me to."

"What matter?"

Looking at me as if he was staring into my soul, he told me, "Naomi, I know something about the fractured nature of the relationship with your father."

"How is it you know about that?"

"He told me. Your father has been a patient in a hospital over in the city for a month now. He has cancer that has metastasized and spread throughout his body. The doctors tell me that with this stage 4 cancer, he has very little time left."

"But when did you talk to him?"

"I went over to the city and visited with him yesterday. He had been shown an article about *All Souls Hospice*. After reading it, he wanted to come back to Holdenville and spend his final days here. The paperwork was finalized, and he'll be admitted as a patient tomorrow. You see, within that article, a brief paragraph mentioned my chaplain's assistant, Naomi Larson."

I had one more question, "What did he say about me?"

Seeing pain in my expression, Stephen came around his desk and sat down in the chair next to mine. Getting closer, he told me, "Naomi, he begged to see you. Of course, I told him that decision would have to be yours. He talked to me at length about his regrets. I believe he wants to ask your forgiveness for the things he said to hurt you."

All the hurt from those sad memories came rushing back, forming into tears filling my eyes. I confessed, "Stephen, I have a lot of complicated feelings about my relationship with my father. It was over ten years ago when my mother died. She was a very religious woman. It was by her life's example I was introduced to Christianity. I so wanted to be like her. I was young and in my last year of high school when she died. It broke my heart. I couldn't handle it or accept it, nor could my father. Her faith was the glue that held us together as a family. With her gone, the relationship with my father started to unravel. He became withdrawn and distant. Somehow, in his mind, he began to blame me for my mother's death. He spoke such words of hate to me that it felt like daggers stuck in my heart."

At this point, Stephen asked, "No matter how bad things were, you didn't try to sit down and talk things out?"

"I was young then and thought our differences were too great to overcome. Looking back on it, I see how deeply depressed he was. It's clear to me now that he was suffering from a broken heart and needed help for his depression. Back then, it was the type of help I didn't know to give him, or get for him. I couldn't cope with what was happening. The rift between us tore our relationship apart. So I left home without telling him, with no thought of ever returning to Holdenville again."

"Did you have any plans? What did you do?"

"No plans. Inside myself, I was lost. I just wandered from state to state, without reason or purpose. Taking odd jobs here and there, I barely survived at times. The days became months, and the months stretched into years. More than ten years passed by."

Noticing my hand was shaking as I relived those dark days, Stephen reached over and closed his hand over mine, calming me. He asked, "During all that time you were lost, what kind of feelings were going through your head?"

"I suppose in the back of my mind, I always felt guilty about not staying home and trying to get my father some kind of help."

"Guilt is a heavy burden for anyone to carry. Most of us have regrets about things we have done or should have done in our lives. That's where the Lord comes in. He can heal us and make us whole again."

"My guilt was one of the reasons I wanted to pray in the chapel when I first came here. God listened and reached inside me, lifting that burden from me. Since I've been at *All Souls*, He's shown me what I can do that is good and decent."

"In doing what is right," Stephen revealed, "I must tell you more of what I've learned in my conversation with your father. After searching for you without success, he finally realized that he had lost you. Knowing he was the cause of you leaving home put a heavy weight of guilt on him. Feeling genuine regret, he sought out counseling and extended psychiatric help. Since those dark days after your mother died, he's made a sincere effort to become a better person. He says he truly wants to be the loving father you once knew."

"What do you think, Stephen?"

"Terminal illness is the one event that brings most everyone closer to God, more so than any other thing in one's life. It's then we realize our own mortality. Many will seek His forgiveness. In those moments, it's up to us to help bring them into communion with our Lord. In your father's case, I saw a lot of sadness on his face throughout our conversation. I think he wants your forgiveness more than anything else."

As I listened to him, so many conflicting feelings went through my head, so I asked, "What should I do?"

"You should search your heart and ask the Lord what you should do. God examines all of us by looking into our souls to see who we really are. You're a good person, Naomi. The Lord will tell you what you must do."

"Then I'll pray about it in my room tonight."

As I started to leave his office, Stephen asked a question that lingered with me, "If Jesus forgave you from the cross, can you do no less?"

Back in my room, those words kept repeating inside my head. I thought about my father a lot that night.

I asked myself, why am I here? Caring for another life is one of the most extraordinarily unselfish things one can do. I believe the Lord brought me here for this reason. There is a great need in this world for a person like me. I'm here now to fulfill that need.

In the midst of all these thoughts running through my mind, I felt a presence just beyond my bed. As I sat up, I saw Sister Mary gazing down at me. She had been silently staring at me, perhaps even reading my mind before she said, "There is something else God wants you to remember."

"What could that be?"

"Something that is very real and already easily accessible within yourself. I'm speaking specifically of the quality of mercy. If you open yourself up to this, its essence will flow out like gentle rain from Heaven and be a part of all you do. Remember, in all things, to thine own self be true. Do this, and you will always be the good person you want to be."

"Sister Mary, I want to do the right thing concerning my father. But what exactly is the right thing?"

"Naomi, listen to me. I will tell you what I know. Jesus wants you to mend what's been broken between you and your father while he still lives."

"It's not an easy thing you ask of me. His last words to me left a deep scar upon my heart."

Her eyes seemed to penetrate my very soul as she spoke, "I see the hurt deep inside you. But I know things about both of you. He loves you, and you still love the father he once was before your mother died. Within you, there's nothing greater than the power of forgiveness, and right now, your father needs to hear that forgiveness from you. He would give anything to have your love back."

I admitted, "I would give anything to have back the

father who loved me."

"My child, the golden rule is at the heart of who you are. Remember, *Do unto others as you would have them do unto you.* Embrace the love and compassion that exists in your soul, and you can do this."

I searched my own consciousness, then I agreed, "Yes, of course, Sister Mary, you're right. To my own self, I must be true." I had reached a decision. I would talk to my father and try to help him find some measure of peace.

The next morning, I went to Chaplain Andrews' office to inform him of my decision, "Stephen, I've decided, I will see my father."

"Naomi, thank you for doing this. He'll be admitted this afternoon. Coming here will be his final journey in this life."

"I'll pray with him and for him, comforting him as much as I can."

"I know you will. I believe, in the process, you will search your own soul, always trying to do and say what is right."

That afternoon I was walking the second-floor hallways thinking about the decision I had made. To see my father, I realized, would be the final act between us. Whatever was said would be permanent for all eternity. So, every word from me would have to be honest and sincere.

As best I could be, I was prepared to reconcile with my father. Standing outside his room, I thought I was ready to see him. Opening the door to his room, I was definitely not prepared for the man I saw...

# CHAPTER 18

# **Forgiveness**

Upon entering my father's room, our eyes met for the first time in over ten years. Neither of us uttered a word. Minutes passed as we just stared at each other.

I thought about our past, what happened between us. I was especially vulnerable after my mom passed away. I had run away from home, from him, because what he said hurt me to the core. But now, the wheels of time had turned. I was no longer a child of those years and had grown into the person I am now. I asked myself, would I be more thoughtful and wise in what I would do now?

For me, it was a shock to see him as he was now. My father had not aged well, as the aggressive stage 4 cancer had taken its toll on him. He looked much older than when I last saw him. His whole body had undergone a long slow deterioration. Before me lay, a man not only broken physically but also broken in spirit. A reflection of the pain he was suffering was deeply etched into his face.

Taking in the fragile state of his entire body, I zeroed in on his right hand as it began to tremble. He was attempting to raise it toward me. Try as he might, he couldn't. In turmoil, tears started to form in his eyes.

Watching him struggle, I thought it's always the right thing to help someone who needs help. Reaching down, I took his hand into mine, gently calming him. I smiled and simply whispered, "It's alright."

Looking up at me from his bed, he finally spoke, "I always wanted you to be like your mother. Now you are." Pausing briefly, as emotions surged through him, then getting a hold of himself, the words came spilling out, "Sometimes I have a hard time communicating, but I need to get this out: I'm so ashamed of myself. There's no excuse for the awful things I said and the way I treated you after your mother died. There has never been a day in the last ten years that I haven't replayed those dark times in my head. If only I could somehow erase what happened between us, I would. If only…"

As he looked up at me, I could see the shame on his face. His eyes seemed to be searching me for some sign of forgiveness.

Answering those silent pleas, I told him what I felt in my heart, "Ten years ago, we both became lost in our grief at the loss of mom. She wouldn't have wanted what has happened between us. We both said and did a lot of things without thinking. With the passage of time, there has been great regret on both our parts. Now, all we can do is try to be better persons to each other."

I could see that he was rolling over every word I had said in his mind. An expression of new resolve formed on his face as he revealed his thoughts, "I can do better than try." He squeezed my hand in a pleading, almost begging manner. His words became even more heartfelt, "I know how deeply I hurt you. My child, is there any way you can find it in your heart to forgive me?"

Looking down at him, I could see my father truly humbled. What he was asking of me was honest and sincere. In my own heart, there was deep regret as well. I, too, wanted forgiveness. Honestly feeling the same need within myself, the words came out of me in a simple whisper, "I forgive you."

As father and daughter, I believe both of us were doing what God would have us do. In reaching out to each other, our two tortured souls had sought and found forgiveness. Years of unresolved feelings between us were replaced by an inner peace that filled our souls. From that day forward, I became my father's daughter again.

When I came into his room the next day, I quickly found my father's thoughts were still about me. Lying there in his bed, his eyes carefully examined me some more before opening up, "Naomi, I've been missing you for so long. Not knowing where you had gone or how to get hold of you, I felt so bad, knowing in my heart I was the one who drove you away. I want to change all of that, beginning today. I want to be the father I should have been years ago." This time, with all the strength he could summon up, he was able to extend a pleading hand toward me.

His words touched my heart again. Reaching down, I took his hand and replied, "Jesus said, *Love one another as I have loved you.* I love you, father."

As he absorbed the impact of my words, his lips trembled, and his eyes started to tear up. Seeing that his feelings were sincere and truly real, I took a long hard look at him. Again, I could see how much the cancer had left him a mere shadow of his former self. I kissed his hand and whispered, "I'll pray for you."

"Before you came today," he said, "I'd been thinking a lot about what I could have and should have been after mom died. So few people ever take the opportunity to review their lives. I saw there was so much wrong in me during the last ten years. I sought out counseling in my journey to try to become a better person. I came to realize so much time has been lost between us."

I reassured him, "The important thing is that I'm here now. We're together, and we will stay together as long as God allows it."

A miracle had happened, something at one time I never thought would've been possible. We were once more joined in a family bond, one that could never be broken now. I knew in my heart we had been reunited in the eyes of the Lord.

More than ever, my father needed me in this the last week he would spend on earth. His decline was rapid. He knew he had only a short time left when I came to his room again. "I'm dying," he said, "maybe not right now or today, but soon. After your mother died, I walked away from God. I don't want to leave this world without setting things right with Him. Naomi, can you help me?"

"What I've learned since coming here is that the Lord is our refuge and our strength. If you open up yourself with a truly repentant heart and welcome His presence into your soul, He will be there for you in your time of need."

"But daughter, when I pray, how will I know God has forgiven me?"

"Just as I do now, you will feel His compassion, His love, and most of all, His presence within you. These are powerful feelings. They redeem us changing the essence of who we are within our own souls. At least, this is how it's been for me. The promise of Heaven can be there for you as well."

"Yes, Naomi, I want it too. Please tell me more about Heaven."

I told him what I believed, "It's in a place beyond the realm of human understanding. Even more so, it is beyond space and time as the mind of man conceives it. Have faith that it exists. Pray about it. Then beyond this life, the Lord will be your guide and show you the reality of Heaven. Once there, you will discover a life that knows no end."

"Daughter, I can honestly say, with all my heart, I want to go there."

"Then pray for His guidance and forgiveness so that one day you will be able to walk through eternity's gate."

My father asked, "Is that how you feel? Is that what you believe?"

"The day I walked through the doors of All Souls back in February, I accepted God into my heart and soul. His presence has been there ever since."

"I know one thing," he added after listening to my every word, "Chaplain Andrews was right."

"Right, about what?"

"When I visited with him at the hospital in the city, he said my daughter truly walked with and talked to the Lord." Going silent, he just looked at me as if he were seeing something he'd never seen before. Then his words expressed what he was thinking, "Naomi, I'm more proud of you than I've ever been. I want to be like you."

"You really mean that, father?"

"Yes, with all my heart."

He seemed so sincere and humble. So I prayed with him and for him. When I left my father's room that evening, I knew for sure the mean spirit that had been in him when I left home was no longer there. Once more, he was becoming the father who raised me, a good man.

From the next morning on, upon entering my father's

room, I could feel the presence of the Lord as well. Looking at me with the eyes of a loving man I had known as a child, he told me what he saw, "I can see it very clearly now. The shadow of Christ is walking with you."

I could see something too, something I kept silent about. My father was nearing the end. Like an awful premonition one never hopes will come true, I saw it all during that day.

Looking up at me, he said, "I've been thinking a lot about death. What do you think?"

"For some, Shakespeare said it best when he described it as the undiscovered country from which no traveler has ever returned. Others, though, down through history have spoken of spirits or guardian angels of sorts, returning with advice and support for the living."

"I'm frightened." My father's voice filled with fear as he expressed his worries, "Sometimes I think I'm not worthy of God's forgiveness because of all I've done and said in my life."

I looked down at my father in his weakened, emaciated state. Barely clinging to life, haunting fears concerning salvation and redemption seized him.

"Father," I said in a calming voice, "remember the presence of the Lord is in this room. Focus on Him, and He will forgive you."

"I want to believe that," he said, calming down. "Naomi, what's going to happen when I die?"

"Here at *All Souls*, I've seen something that has happened more than once when one gets close to death. The patient sees and hears things no one else can."

"Daughter, is that really true?"

"It's true. A few of our patients enter into a state where I believe God enables them to see loved ones from the other side, or angles and a glimpse of Heaven before passing into it."

"What does it all mean?" My father asked, wanting to know more.

"It means Heaven *IS* real. When Jesus said, *I am with you always*, He meant it. God is the ultimate reality for all who open up their minds to Him."

An expression of pride formed on his face as he spoke, "My child, you've grown into a wise woman. As you go on, doing good things in your life, I feel like a little bit of the best of me will still be living in you."

While we were talking, my father was struggling to get his breath. The necessary oxygen to sustain his life was coming far too slowly. Life was quickly ebbing from him. Squeezing my hand, he whispered, "I'm so very sorry…." His voice trailed off into silence as his eyes closed for a final time.

Complete quiet settled over the room. Not another word was spoken between us. A sense of eternal peace, the kind only God could give, filled the room.

We both had wanted more time. Sadly, though, this was not to be. Death's shadow was no longer to be denied.

My father took one last deep breath, then let it out very

slowly. After that, he simply stopped breathing. It seemed like every organ in his body shut down all at once. The life essence within him was no more.

I stood looking down at my father. Only his body's empty shell remained. His soul had already gone with God.

I was not alone in my father's room now. Putting a comforting hand on my shoulder, Ann Bishop had come up beside me. She whispered, "Naomi, my friend, the Lord has taken your father home."

"Ann, I just wanted a little more time with him. This may sound strange, but I wish that somehow I could've walked a little way with my father on his road to eternity."

"Not strange at all," Ann reasoned, "I think we all wish we could have a little more time with our lost loved ones. I miss my dad a lot. He died way too young. But you know, when I try really hard, I can still hear some of the nice things he said to me when he was alive."

"Thank you for saying that. You're a good friend."

"I've been watching you," Ann confessed, "all these past several months since Ruth died. You've been giving from your heart to so many. In doing so, you've been giving hope to those who needed it most. I admire you for that."

"I was just doing what God wanted me to do."

"I think it has become much more than that for you. Giving of yourself to others has become a way of life for you. From Chaplain Andrews on down, we have noticed how you lift people up, helping all those who need help."

"Yes," I admitted, "my work here has become much more than just a job. From Timmy and Ruth to many others, and now my father, I loved them with all the love in my heart. And now…"

Tears were forming in my eyes as my heart was filling with emotion. Ann could see this. As if she knew, she completed my thoughts, "And now their spirits are very much alive with our Father in Heaven. Yet, in doing so, you've helped make *All Souls* a healing place for so many."

"A healing place." I repeated her words, thinking of how I felt inside myself at that very moment, "Perhaps it's from losing my father and all the others you mentioned, I feel overwhelmed with grief. I feel like I need help now. I'm hurting inside myself. What do you think I should do?"

"I know what you should do." Ann responded with great confidence in her voice, "You reminded me of it when I needed help."

Feeling so drained and worn down, I couldn't think. So, I asked, "What did I tell you?"

"You told me to go to God in prayer. You said seek answers from Him."

It was then I realized how drained out I was. I'd been pushing myself way too hard, taking care of my father and the other patients as well. Getting little or no sleep at all, I had pushed myself to the brink of exhaustion.

"Ann, I'll say it again, you're a really good friend, the one I needed the most right now." Giving her a hug, I said,

"Thanks to you, I know what to do now."

Turning to leave my father's room, she called after me, "Naomi, where are you going?"

"Upstairs, where I can look up at the heavens and seek answers from Him."

Even then, while waiting for the elevator to the third floor, I had the glimmer of a thought that something just ahead of me might change my life once more.

# CHAPTER 19

# Into The Light

I walked out of the elevator into the third-floor family room. Just ahead of me, I collapsed into the nearest chair. Weighted down with a lot of sorrow churning around inside myself, it had hit me quite suddenly after my father's death.

I was all alone in the large room, sitting there in complete silence. Many thoughts were rushing through my brain, one right after another. I could help almost anyone here at *All Souls*, but right now, I couldn't help myself. All the turmoil swirling around inside me brought tears to my eyes.

It was then, in the midst of my grief, I suddenly realized a gentle hand had rested itself on my shoulder, comforting me. Its warmth calmed me. Conscious of it, my eyes went up the owner's arm into her face. It was Sister Mary.

I explained, "My father is gone. I didn't know it would hit me this hard. After my mother passed away, I was not ready to accept it for a long time. Now my father has died, and I'm not sure I can deal with it. I just can't process it in my head."

"Of course, you can, child. Don't you understand what God has done? In His infinite wisdom, He has taken away the old conflict that still existed, deep down between you and your father. He has brought you both peace. And now, he is out of pain from the cancer, and his soul is with the Lord in Heaven."

I felt a measure of inner peace. Her words always had a positive effect on me. Yet, there was still something bothering me. "Sister Mary, you've helped me so much, but there is something inside me still, tearing at my soul. I've lost little Timmy, Ruth Wilson, and so many others I've loved here. I feel completely drained out. I'm not sure what it is, but I've lost something I need back."

"Naomi, we are all on a path that God sets us upon. Sometimes we need Him more than we think. All those you've loved here have gone home to the Lord. Sometimes the reality that they are gone from this life leaves us with an acute sense of loss that is hard to deal with. Remember, you can always go to Jesus in prayer, and He will be there with open arms to comfort your heart and soul."

"I wish I could go to Him right now." Even as I said it, tears were welling up in my eyes. I felt such a collective weight of sadness inside me that it left me shaken.

Sister Mary's eyes searched me far more than skin deep

and saw it too. She explained, "I have seen this before in others much stronger than you. I want you to stop suffering. Maybe you should see Jesus again."

"Yes, now more than ever," I pleaded.

Again, Sister Mary studied me closely. "Sometimes, things in life impact us beyond all reason. I know of a time when many who were profoundly strong had their faith shaken. Then Christ came to them. If you go to Him, perhaps He can heal all that's wrong within you as well."

"I'm sure of it. That's what I want, with all my heart."

"Then, my child, stare straight ahead. Concentrate, and you will see a light forming in front of your eyes. Keep your eyes fixed on it."

It was a small dot of light at first. Expanding rapidly, it grew more intense by the second. Forming into a swirling mass, it quickly became what I felt was spiritual energy. Drawing me into a realm of total light, there was no turning back now.

Whatever was taking place, I knew my guardian angel had something to do with it. I called out, "Sister Mary, what's happening?"

"You're on a path through the light. It's also a path to the healing process."

"What happens there?"

"This is where one opens up one's heart to God, seeking His help."

"Is it that simple?"

"Simple for some, difficult for others. For you must open up your whole heart and soul to the Lord. For some, it's remarkably easy. For others, overcoming one's self-pride and opening up to someone greater than any mortal man, someone they cannot see, is unacceptable. Many who don't know God do not want to accept Him."

While we were talking, I pushed on through the endless path into the light. Seeming like forever, I asked, "Sister Mary, where am I going?"

"You're going to the little village of Emmaus, seven miles west of Jerusalem. Only it's 2,000 years ago. You're in the home of Cleopas and his wife, who were present at the crucifixion of Christ."

"Why were they there?"

"Cleopas was the younger brother of Joseph, the foster-father of Jesus. Due to mob violence and Christian persecution in Jerusalem, their home in Emmaus became a safe house for the disciples of Jesus. As you arrive, most of them are gathered in an upstairs room."

"Why was Emmaus so safe? Please tell me more about this little village."

"Emmaus was a special place in the eyes of the Lord and Jewish history. The Ark of the Covenant was kept there for many decades before being moved to Jerusalem by King David. Many Christians lived there. They felt safe because it was a walled village, garrisoned by elements of the Tenth Roman Legion, charged with keeping the peace. There is evidence many soldiers stationed there were present during the sermon on the mount and were converted to Christianity."

"Fascinating, I did not know these things."

"There are many biblical stories that have been lost through the centuries."

Getting back to what was happening, I announced, "I'm in the house now, at the foot of a steep staircase, leading to a closed door beyond."

"Go ahead, Naomi, climb the stairs, and enter the room. You are carrying a large tray of fruit and bread prepared by Cleopas and his wife. The apostles of Jesus are hungry and have not eaten. They will welcome you in the room where they are gathered."

I wondered aloud, "But, why am I here?"

Sister Mary's voice answered, "All of your questions will soon be answered."

On my way up the stairs, I felt the after-effects of the intense light I had journeyed through in getting here. I had been left feeling a sense of having been cleansed by its energy. Something inside me was urging me on, telling me this was the right thing to do. As I entered the large room, I knew immediately that the spirit of Christ was there also.

Getting everyone's attention, I let them all know, "I bring fruit and bread from the house of Cleopas." Sitting the tray down on a nearby table, everyone seemed to gather around it.

Turning around, I noticed a lone figure standing just

inside the door, over in a nearby shadowy corner. I felt compelled to go over to him, his energy beckoning to me. It was the same energy I had felt in the rooms of dying patients at *All Souls*.

As I got closer, I still could not see his face even though I knew he was staring at me. Then, still nearer, I stood right in front of him. He lowered the cowl covering His face. It was Him. For the second time in my life, I was staring into the face of Jesus. I whispered, "My Lord and my God."

After that, not a word passed between us as He looked at me, His eyes peering right into my soul. In that same instant, I was transfixed by His gaze. I saw the goodness and purity that made Him the son of God. Then I saw something greater. It was an internal light made visible, something all-powerful. For me, it was the light of eternal life.

Breaking His silence, He extended His hand toward me and whispered, "Naomi, remember, I said from the cross, I am with you always. I will never leave you or forsake you. Listen when I speak to the others. You need to hear it as well." His voice was the same voice I had heard from the cross, but this time its warmth and healing were directed to me. In physical appearance, He was healed. The scars of crucifixion were still there but faded. The places where he had been bruised and bloodied were gone, healed by Almighty God.

Suddenly, as if He saw or heard something I didn't, He backed into the shadows again. He was still there but couldn't be seen by the others. Our solitary moment was about to be intruded upon by the rest of those present.

In that same instant, feeling like I was the object of someone else's gaze, I looked around. From across the room, young John had recognized me as the woman he had met at Christ's crucifixion. His eyes followed me as I started to move from the corner of the room. Moving closer, he stopped right in front of me, revealing his thoughts, "It's you, you're here. I don't know who you are, but you're a good person."

"Now, how do you know that?" I wondered how he arrived at that conclusion.

"Remember, we spoke at the crucifixion. I saw those qualities in you there. You're a rare person."

"How so?"

"Because you're so visibly spiritual. It's rare that one sees it so clearly in others. But then too, you knew my Master was the son of God."

"John, He's my Master as well."

"Then, what brings you here?"

"Because the chains of death could not hold Him. Jesus is in this room right now. John, look over my shoulder. He's standing in the shadows right behind me. I think He wants to speak to all of you."

I stepped aside while Jesus emerged from the shadows again. The other disciples turned and looked. Some were frightened, even terrified. All were amazed. Extending His arms, Jesus calmed them at once, "Be not afraid, peace be unto all of you, my children. Though dead, I have risen and am alive, now and forever. I am neither spirit nor ghost. Just as much as all of you are, I am flesh and bones." Looking around the room, Jesus noticed one disciple was missing. "Where is Thomas?"

Peter spoke up, "He lingered in Jerusalem, defending you to all who opposed you. But he told me he would meet us here this day."

Going to his knees in front of Jesus, John asked, "What's going to happen, Master?"

Reaching out, touching his forehead, Jesus answered, "No matter what happens, I will be with you right here, even unto the end of the world."

Just then, there was a knock at the door. Once again, Jesus stepped back into the shadowy corner, out of immediate sight.

Going to the door, Peter opened it to let in the missing disciple. Closing the door behind himself, Thomas explained, "I've just come from Jerusalem, barely escaping with my life. The mob is still worked up, wanting to stone all who have believed in Jesus. I have heard some stories that He has risen from the dead, but I haven't seen Him. I wonder, could it be true?"

Quickly, Peter answered, "It is true! We have all seen Him."

Thomas looked at Peter, still somewhat skeptical. "I would like to believe it, but unless I see where the nails went into His flesh and unless I touch where the Roman spear pierced His side, I will not believe."

John came forward, getting directly in front of Thomas, confronting him, "You will have your chance, for Jesus is in this room at this very moment."

All of the disciples gathered around Thomas as they turned and directed their focus on the shadowy corner behind him. Now, Thomas also turned and looked in the same direction.

Emerging from the dark corner again, Jesus came forward until He stood right in front of His doubting disciple. "Thomas, you said you wanted to see." He held out His arms, so the holes made by the nails impaling Him to the cross were clearly visible. Then He opened His robe, revealing the massive wound made by the puncture of the Roman spear. "Go ahead, put your finger into my side. Touch it, Thomas."

Hesitant at first, I could see many thoughts running through the doubting disciple's head. Reaching forward, he touched the horrible wound. I could see it in his face: realizing Jesus had risen from the dead, tears formed in Thomas's eyes. I could see he felt ashamed for his doubt. Going to his knees, it was as if his soul had been laid open and all of his emotions were visible. Words came from a place deep within his heart as he acknowledged, "My Lord and my God." He could say no more, crying aloud.

Jesus looked down at him with compassion. Leaning forward, He wrapped His arms around Thomas, consoling him with His love. "Blessed are you, Thomas, for revealing who I am. Blessed are all of you who have believed, and to all who have not seen but yet believe I am the son of God."

Looking up into the face of Jesus, Thomas asked, "Master, what shall we do? We are few against so many non-believers. How shall we fight them?"

"You will not fight them. Blessed are the peacemakers, for they shall be called the children of God. Love your enemies. Do good to those who hate you. Bless those who curse you. Pray for those who mistreat and persecute you. Do these things, and you will truly be the children of your Father, who is in Heaven."

Peter, who had been listening intently, spoke up, "Master, not a day passes that we don't need your advice and counsel. We are not as strong as you are."

Jesus looked into Peter's face and the faces of all the others, telling them what He saw, "Peter, you are so full of courage. You're a rock. I am the good shepherd to all of you here. You, my disciples, are the stones of Israel. Together, all of you form an unbreakable rock. It is upon this rock, that you will be the foundation of my church to the rest of the world. I say unto all of you, I will strengthen you and be with you always."

"But Master," young John pleaded, "won't you stay and help us?"

"John, I must go to my Father's house and prepare a place for all of you and all who will believe in me. In my

Father's house, Heaven is a vast place of many mansions. One day we will all be together again. When that day comes, I will be standing there with open arms to greet you and all who have believed in me. I promise."

At this point, Peter put into words what all were feeling in that room, "We love you, Master."

Jesus extended His hand to all of us who were gathered as if to bless us all. "I say to all of you, love one another as I have loved you."

Following up on that, John asked, "What else do you want us to do?"

"I charge you, all of you, go unto all the world, preaching the gospel to every creature, to those of all nations. Make disciples of all those who believe, baptizing them in the name of the Father, the Son, and the Holy Spirit."

Absorbing every word Jesus said, realizing his whole life was about to change once more, Thomas asked the most profound question we all might ask, "Master, when we do all that you have charged us with, what will happen when we die."

Jesus looked deeply into his heart and the hearts of all of us, then answered, "I am the resurrection and the life. He who believes in me will live. Even though one dies, you will have everlasting, eternal life with me in Heaven."

Thomas was moved, as were all of us, yet he still wondered, "Until that time, when I see you again, Master, will I be alone?"

"You will not be alone, Thomas. I say unto all of you, though I will be in another place, I will hear all of your prayers and be an ever-present help to you in all of your needs. If you open up your hearts when you pray, you will hear my voice within yourselves."

I could see love and compassion in Christ's face that went far and beyond anything I'd ever seen. At the same time, I could see it in the faces of all the disciples gathered there on their knees, entranced before Jesus. Giving His love to them helped the morale within each and every one of them. That night, Christ healed the fear and hurt within their minds. Even more importantly, though, He gave them some of His own inner strength. To a man, they were built up to the point where they would all give their lives for Him.

It was a moment that strengthened me as well. Even then, I knew this was another defining moment in my life. I felt cleansed of all my sorrows and lifted up by the presence of Christ.

In the very next moment, as we all felt the love radiating from Him, Jesus became transparent and vanished. Yet, though He was gone from the room, in the minds and hearts of all of us present, He had been there.

For me, in my mind, He will always be there. For long afterward, and even today, I remember Jesus whispering to me. His words will be engraved upon my heart forever.

Looking into the faces of all the disciples, I could see they were all equally affected by Christ's presence and what they saw and heard. Their faith was restored. They now had a renewed sense of purpose in their lives. They could now move mountains. They did. In the course of doing it, the world was changed forever.

Nearest to me had been young John. Seeing his facial reaction, I knew that the love of Jesus would sustain him all the rest of his life. Yet, as he returned my gaze, our eyes connected, and something else happened. Something unspoken passed between us. Before I could avoid him, he was standing in front of me again. Knowing it for sure, that somehow we were on the same wavelength, he said, "I can see it, feel it in you. Some of my Master's spiritual energy is in you."

"Yes, it's true," I admitted, "I believe every living soul in this room has been changed by what we saw and heard from the son of God today."

"You knew who He was. My Master saw you at the cross. I saw it in His eyes as well. He knew you." As he went on, I could tell his curiosity was getting the best of him. It came to a head when he blurted out, "I must know! Just who are you?"

"Just someone who also loves Jesus." Immediately I could tell my quick answer was not sufficient, so I tried to elaborate, "From the first time I heard your Master's words, I knew He was the son of God. Ever since then, I've been a follower. My name is…"

Before I could tell young John my name, I felt the powerful light I was quite familiar with by now surround me in that same instant. Pulling my mind and conscious thought from that room of long ago, I found myself back in the chair in front of Sister Mary. It was like I had been in a vivid, all too real dream. Or perhaps, I had been plunged into a vision, one of my guardian angel's making this time.

I started explaining to her what had happened, "The last thing I saw was the kind and understanding face of young John expecting to know my name. Before I could tell him, I was pulled back to the present."

Sister Mary explained, "It was not meant for John to know your name, at least then." Before I could respond, she quickly moved on to an important question, "Having seen Jesus again, how do you feel?"

"I feel strengthened by His words. They are inside me, continuing to heal, even now. Feeling His presence has put my mind at peace again. Yet, I feel strangely exhausted."

"That is as it should be, my child. You've seen and experienced something in a way no one else has. What you saw and heard was what God wanted to reveal to your mind alone. It was beyond mankind's understanding of the dimensions of space and time."

"It was a miracle."

"Yes, Naomi. It was a miracle for you so that you might be strengthened in your faith once again."

"Sister Mary, just the thought of the experience will inspire me for the rest of my life."

"Oh, my child, many other things will happen over the

course of your life that inspire you and change you as you grow in understanding."

"I saw the apostles grow in understanding while I was there. What happened to them after I left?"

"Mostly, they stayed among friends and Christians in Emmaus for the coming weeks until the end of forty days. Then Jesus called them all together on the Mount of Olives, a mountain ridge that overlooked Jerusalem from the East. It was from there, Jesus ascended into Heaven before more than 500 witnesses. Among them were many Roman soldiers from the 10th Legion, garrisoned in Emmaus."

"How is it I've never heard of Emmaus?"

"Perhaps it's because in the last 2,000 years, Emmaus was lost, its whereabouts unknown to modern historians. That was until a 2017 archaeological expedition, a joint venture of Tel Aviv University and the College de France, began to rediscover its exact location. By 2019, the dig had yielded finds from the ancient village, including Roman tiles from the garrison, coins, and pro-Christian articles carried by soldiers who had secretly converted to Christianity. The coins containing the image of the Roman emperor, Caligula, had been slashed across the face. His brief four-year reign from 37 to 41 AD was the first persecution of Christians by a Roman emperor. The soldiers-who were Christians defaced his image on coins as a sign of their feelings against him."

"History and the truth is so interesting from one who knows," I acknowledged what Sister Mary knew.

Continuing her narrative, she told me, "The lives of all the apostles changed from the day they saw the risen Christ in the house of Cleopas. They all became unafraid and gave their lives for Christ in the days and years after that.

I wondered, "What happened to Thomas who had doubted Him that day?"

"He promised Jesus he would be a witness for Him until the day he died. He kept that promise, going into what is now Afghanistan, Iran, and on to India, where he became a pastor of Christ's church there. It was there he was murdered by a mob, receiving a fatal spear wound in almost the same place as Jesus did on the cross."

"In a way, it was his destiny," I added.

"Just as all of the apostles had destinies in their time, so do we have destinies to fulfill in our time. Right now, my child, how do you feel about yourself?"

"Being so close to Jesus, some of His energy has filled my heart and soul, making me whole again."

She smiled and reflected, "What better a place to receive healing than at the feet of the Master Himself. Before I go, I wanted to say one more thing to you. Naomi, I'm so very proud of you. I will love you, always and forever."

I asked, "Do you suppose, one day we might know each other in Heaven?"

She smiled and answered, "Of course we will."

Almost as an afterthought, I asked something I had to know, "You never said, what happened to young John?"

"Like the others, he journeyed throughout the known world, spreading the word of Jesus unafraid. Unlike all the others, he passed away from natural causes in his old age. There was something else, though."

"What was that?"

"He was always searching for someone or something. Even when asked, he never said."

"Do you know who he was looking for?"

She just sort of smiled, looking directly at me. Then she said something very strange, "Sometimes, in our dreams or visions, we find our destinies." As I thought about that in silence for a moment, Sister Mary smiled again and vanished.

Finding myself all alone in the third-floor family room, I stared out the large picture window. It was getting dusk out. Going over to the large sofa facing it, I flipped on a nearby table lamp. Total exhaustion hitting me, I slumped down on the sofa. I felt drained out from all that had happened that day. Yet I still wanted to pray. I thanked God for making me feel whole again. Though invisible to human eyes, I believe I will always feel His presence.

I thought, who knows who I might meet on my journey through this life? If that one single person cried out for help, what would I do? For some unknown reason, that question lingered in my mind as I fell asleep on the sofa.

# CHAPTER 20

# A Promise

The next thing I knew, it was several hours later. Though I hadn't meant to, I had slept most of the night on the sofa in the third-floor family room.

Night and the silence that goes with it were gone. Even though it was not yet daylight, I could hear birds waking and chirping in the far distance. The sounds of a few isolated vehicles could also be heard, but far away. The town was waking up to a new day, yet morning had not quite broken yet.

Sitting up, from my view out the picture window, I focused on the eastern horizon. A red aura was trying to poke itself into view. It made me think of God, that He is the light of the world, only with a different kind of light, a spiritual light.

The results of my concentration revealed a unique picture to my eyes. It seemed as though every atom contained many variations of warm colors beamed across the morning horizon. The rays took shape as a fiery, reddish orb and rose into the morning sky.

I sat there motionless, appreciating every second of it. This was a new day for me because I saw things clearer than I ever had. I whispered, "If only I'd ever really looked before. I have seen your face in front of me, Lord. I've seen You every morning, without realizing it was you. One day You really will make the world anew."

The brilliance of His light brought tears to my eyes, while its warmth uplifted my heart and soul. Each day God's presence is all around us, and we don't see it. Nature holds so much beauty from the Lord if only we would open our eyes to it.

I spoke to Him once more, "Right now, I'm not wanting to ask for anything, but to simply give my thanks for all that You've blessed me with."

Just then, something came over me, like a premonition. I could feel it coming, something that would signal the beginning of a new chapter in my life. I took this feeling very seriously. After the events of yesterday, I knew, that for people of faith, all things are possible unto the Lord.

Sensing the presence of someone close by, I looked around to see Chaplain Andrews standing in the doorway. "I know it's early," he said, "but I had to see you. I'm sorry about your father's passing yesterday, and ordinarily, I wouldn't bother you with this right now, but the situation demands that I speak to you about it."

"Yes, of course. What is it?"

"We have an early morning visitor requesting to see you."

I was surprised, "To see me? Who would want to see me?"

"It's Ruth Wilson's son, Sergeant Wilson. He's been discharged. It seems he's leaving the army. Departing from Bagram Air Base in Afghanistan, he recently arrived back in the United States. He came here because he felt it important."

"To see me?" I repeated the question, still not quite believing someone would make a special trip to see me.

"Naomi, sometimes the little things you do mean an awful lot to others. Before she passed away, Ruth wrote her son a letter."

"Yes, I remember. I mailed it for her."

"In that letter," Chaplain Andrews explained, "she spoke very highly of you. He said that since you meant so much to his mother, he simply had to meet you."

I asked, "Is that what he really said?"

"As I visited with him in my office," Stephen offered his impressions of Sergeant Wilson, "I found that he'd been through a lot in Afghanistan. I could still see the pain in his face. He saw a lot of killing and other horrible things over there. I think inside that he's still suffering. He said one of the things that got him through it was being able to read his Bible whenever he could."

"I'm glad God's word helped get him through it all."

"Even more important, when he received the letter you mailed to him, hearing that someone good and decent like yourself was taking care of his mother, it raised his morale. He said it made him feel good that there was still somebody like you in this old world."

This moved me and, at the same time, frightened me just a little. "Stephen, do you think I can measure up to that? What do you think I should do?"

"I know you can. Remember this, you reap what you sow. What you've sown here at *All Souls* has been a harvest in abundance. You've woven the threads of goodness, inspiring faith into the lives of those who needed it the most."

"Have I really done all of that?"

"Yes, you have. Think about it. You've always told me you were trying to become a better person. Over the past ten months, you've become that person. Looking inside yourself, think this above all, to thine own self be true. If you know what that is, the best version of yourself, you already know what you should do. For you, there is true wisdom in following your own heart."

I searched myself, taking in every word Stephen was saying. Acknowledging it, I said, "There's truth in everything you said."

"One thing more," Stephen added, "remember he's Ruth's son. Didn't you promise her you'd meet with him if he ever came here?"

"Yes, I did."

"I think, after all this young man has been through, he deserves our understanding. I believe he's a little lost inside, crying for help."

There were those words, *crying for help*. "I was thinking those very words last night."

"What?" He didn't understand.

"Oh, I was thinking about what I would do if I could help someone. Yes, of course, I'll meet with him and do my best to help."

"Good, I believe in my heart this is the right thing for you to do. He's still in my office downstairs. I'll send him up on the elevator shortly."

I reassured him, "I'll be right here, waiting."

Deep down, I thought, in some strange way, this has something to do with my destiny. When I came here, I was lost, and the Lord helped me. Perhaps it was now my turn to help someone else. Whatever I would need to do, He would point the way.

While I was waiting, I sat there staring out the picture window, thinking of Ruth and the promise I made to her. It had been a solemn promise to someone I had grown to love, a sacred commitment to a dying soul. By fulfilling this promise, I was reaffirming my love for Ruth. Even so, something inside myself made me feel uneasy. I didn't know what it was. I whispered, "Please help me, Lord."

The Lord heard me and would soon answer my plea. In

a few moments, I heard the elevator doors open out in the hall. Very soon, something would happen that would change my world and my life forever.

# CHAPTER 21

# He Works In Mysterious Ways

While waiting on Sergeant Wilson, I got up from the sofa and went over by the sliding glass doors leading to the rooftop patio. Staring out across the eastern horizon, I took in the early morning view as many thoughts ran through my head.

I had put my whole heart and soul into my work since coming here ten months ago. I was ready to engage others with the very best version of myself. I was the person God wanted me to be. I was ready to talk to Ruth's son. Or was I?

Something unsettling ran through my mind. I went to my knees. Breaking my view of the sky just beyond the glass doors, I bowed my head to pray. I couldn't, though. Something was still firmly lodged in my mind. Sister Mary had said earlier, that sometimes in our dreams or visions, we find our destinies. I asked her, "What did you mean by that?"

Her voice spoke to my mind, answering, *You have to meet Ruth's son. He is your past as well as your future.*

"I don't understand. What do you mean?"

*All will become clear when you meet Sergeant Wilson. Remember what I have often said, God works in mysterious ways.*

"Sister Mary?" Silence. Her spirit and her voice had left the family room. I was alone again.

Still kneeling on the floor, trying to pray, I whispered, "God, please help me to say the right thing to Ruth's son." After another moment of long silence, I heard the elevator doors open out in the hall and footsteps growing louder behind me. One last time I whispered, "Lord, please help me. Thy will be done in all things."

Just then, a voice spoke up behind me, "Yes, may His will be done in all things." His voice sounded strangely familiar as he continued, "I'm sorry, I didn't mean to interrupt your prayer, Miss Naomi."

"You know my name?"

"Yes, from Chaplain Andrews. Also, my mother mentioned it in her last letter to me. I'm Sergeant Wilson. As soon as it was possible, I wanted to meet the lady who treated my mom so nice and gave her so much love in her last days."

"Sergeant, it was my honor to take care of your mother. She was truly a great lady."

"It's my honor also, just to meet you. Miss Naomi, I would like very much to talk with you a bit. Please, let me help you up."

Up to now, Sergeant Wilson had been standing a few feet behind me. Coming up alongside me, he extended his hand down into my eye level. Even as I took it, there was something oddly familiar about his hand as well.

Standing up slowly, my long hair obscured a full view of my face. Coming to my feet, my eyes took in his uniform. Then I saw his face. His features startled me. I asked myself, could it be true? Except for the shorter hair, the sergeant looked remarkably like John the Apostle! Awed by his appearance, I haltingly asked, "Now, again, who are you?"

"I'm John, John Wilson."

Brushing my hair back, John got his first unobstructed look at my face. He became very quiet, his eyes studying me carefully, realizing I was who he thought I was.

Actually, for a moment, we were both silent, just staring at each other. I believe we were both thinking, was the impossible possible?

He looked at me like it was for the first time, though it really wasn't, as he indicated when he finally spoke, "I met you in my dreams."

Seeing that he was visibly struggling to make sense of it made me want to help him even more, "I've often heard that dreams have a meaning. Sometimes we encounter people in our dreams that we might one day really meet. You were in the visions I was having. In them, you were as real as you are here."

John started sharing his own feelings, "At first, I thought the mystery woman in my dreams was a figment of my imagination. Then you started seeming so real. Your image haunted me. I tried to wrap my head around the possibility that the souls of the living could meet in dreams. The more I thought about it, I felt like I was being condemned to chasing after a ghost that was only alive in my dreams. So I ask you the same question you asked me, who are you?"

"I'm just an assistant to Chaplain Andrews."

Searching my face, his thoughts became words, "I think you're much more than that." Yet again, he asked me again, with even more insistence, "Just who are you, really?"

His question reached straight into my heart for a more complete answer. I opened up about myself, "I'm nothing without the Lord in my life. With Him, I'm everything. I've put my whole heart and soul into my work here."

"I know that you have," he observed. "I see it in your face. You know God as few people will ever get to know Him."

"John, how do you know this?"

"Chaplain Andrews said you were a person who had experienced God's miracles in your life. My mother's letter spoke of what a good person you were that you seemed to have the spirit of the Lord within you. Remember, we were together in your visions and my dreams, both of us being in the presence of Jesus Christ as few people ever were or will be. Beyond all of that, I feel His presence in the energy you project."

Looking into his penetrating, understanding eyes, I confirmed what he was saying, "Yes, all that you say is true. I feel God's presence within me every single day of my life."

"Then please," he urged, "help me make sense of what happened, how our souls have become connected. What does it all mean?"

"It means that God is involved in our lives far more than we realize. We are all His children. On that level–His level–we are all interconnected."

"Yes, I'm beginning to understand." John seemed to comprehend what I was telling him. Yet, he wanted to know more. "We both had vivid dreams or visions of the same events, each from our own perspectives. But, for what purpose?"

I understood this part, "It was God's purpose, His involvement in our lives. A dear old friend of mine, I'll call her my guardian angel, often told me that God works in mysterious ways. I'm beginning to understand the full meaning of that now."

John looked at me as if his mind was opening up to this possibility as he accepted God's hand at work here, "Whatever the reason, I think it was a miracle, God's miracle in both our lives. For whatever reason, I'm very glad to know you, Naomi Larson."

"I'm very glad to know you too, John Wilson."

Being far from finished, he reached out to me further, "I would like very much to share something else with you, that is if you have the time."

"My time is your time."

We went back over to the sofa. Sitting there, John began, "It means so much to me, actually more than I can put into words. You were here for my mother. I'd like to tell you what I'm thinking."

"Yes, John, please tell me what you're thinking."

He gently took my hand and proceeded to open up his heart, "In her last days, you gave my mother hope and love from the goodness in your soul. I think you're a very special person to do that."

"I loved your mother, John."

Tears formed in his eyes as he whispered, "Bless you, Naomi, forever and ever. When I got the news my mother had passed, it felt like a part of me was ripped away, gone forever."

"She's not gone," I explained from my own experience, "Whenever you think of your mother, as long as you keep her alive in your mind, her spirit will be with you, often with words of wisdom for your soul."

John's expression became more positive.

I asked, "What is it?"

"I just remembered, Chaplain Andrews told me how very close you were to my mother."

"Your mother was a kind, loving woman. She told me how she would read the Bible to you as a child."

"It was because of her that I continued to read the Bible as I grew up. When I got to Afghanistan, it seemed death was around every corner. I saw so many people killed. It made me stop and think, how does God feel about all the killing and endless wars?"

I told him what Jesus said, "*All who take up the sword will die by the sword.* Jesus also said something about those that spread peace and goodwill among mankind, *Blessed are the peacemakers, for they shall be called the children of God.* All life is precious to the Lord."

John remembered what was still vivid in his mind, "I saw such loss of hope in the faces of many little children who had been scared and made orphans by the war. What I saw motivated me to read the Bible every chance I got. I remembered that Jesus had said something about every life ever lived had something of value to the Lord. So I started reading about the life of Christ and His apostles as often as I could. Then I started having vivid dreams that I was young John the Apostle. I listened and learned from Jesus, hearing Him speaking to me. It was so real, as though I was actually there. Now I feel closer to the Lord than at any time in my life."

"I believe that's why you had those dreams. Jesus wanted you to know Him, even if it was in dreams."

Absorbing that thought, it was like a lightbulb turned

on in John's head. "What I experienced was more than mere dreams. They were something deeper, actually spiritual experiences. They awakened something within me that affected my life and made me want to survive in Afghanistan. What was it like for you, Naomi?"

"At first, I questioned if I should even be having visions. But, as I studied the Bible, I learned that God had communicated with many people through visions over centuries, throughout both the Old and New Testaments. After my visions, I felt His Holy Spirit surrounding me, healing me, making me a better person."

John added, "I had similar feelings after my dreams. It felt like God comforted me, healing me from the inside, where I had become broken by the war. One last thing though, how is a dream different than a vision?"

"I believe they are remarkably the same. The only difference is a vision occurs while one is awake. Dreams occur when one is asleep. A dream is but a vision of the night, or so it says in the book of Job. In both, I feel God is communicating with us, speaking directly to our souls, in the way He sees best."

John thought about it, "The day God started speaking to my soul was the day I started becoming a better person."

"Now you see where God has led you," I pointed out. "Here we are, sitting on this sofa, talking to each other, reaching a clearer understanding about all that brought us here."

"Thinking about all that has happened to me," John

recalled, "in a strange way, seeing the world's evil in war had something to do with it. So many have forgotten what Jesus told all of us, *Love thy neighbor as thy self.* If more people practiced that one commandment, perhaps it would be a major step toward a better world."

"Maybe, John, you might be one of those who will help change the way people think. You might just become one of those peacemakers Jesus was talking about."

"Me? Well, I do wonder what I'll do with the rest of my life, now that I'm getting out of the military."

"Your mother told me once when you came home, she hoped you would go on to have a good life, a fulfilled life. I would often hear her pray that the Lord would be with you and guide you in whatever you do."

John looked at me admiringly. "Naomi, I'm deeply humbled just to know you. You're a truly good person. Bless you, for who you are."

As I listened to him, I could see the honesty in his face and hear the sincerity in his voice. So, I told him how I felt, "I'm humbled too, that God has allowed me to come to know you."

"I really want to be the man you think I am and become the man my mother wanted me to be. I can think of one thing I immediately want to do."

"What is that?"

"Naomi, would you pray with me and for me?"

"Of course, I will." I put both my hands together like

praying hands and began with words I've always felt deeply about, some from the 23rd Psalm, "The Lord is my shepherd, I shall not want, for He leadeth me through my life, restoring my soul. Though I walk through the valley of the shadow of death, I will fear no evil, for You are with me. Your Holy Spirit will comfort me. Your goodness and mercy will be with me all the rest of my days. At the end of my life, I will go with You and dwell in the house of the Lord, forever."

I looked up into John's face. It was full of emotion, with tears forming in his eyes. Reaching for my hand, he gently kissed it. As his eyes met mine again, he shared his thoughts, "I feel the arc of my whole life changing. I'm beginning to think where my future might lead me, from being a soldier in war to becoming something else."

I asked, "What would that be?"

"Becoming a Christian soldier in the service of God."

I admired him for saying that and thought of Ruth, "Your mother would be very proud to hear you say those words. You know, I think somehow she knows."

I could see a pleading expression on his face as he reached out to me, asking, "Naomi, would you help me become that Christian soldier?"

"Of course, I will." I felt like I was fulfilling a sacred promise I had made to Ruth. I could see that our conversation had inspired her son to a new higher purpose in his life.

With so many life-changing thoughts going through his head, he focused on his need to discuss things with me,

"There's so much more I would like to talk to you about. If only there were more time."

"There is time," I answered. "We can talk more if you wish."

"On my way up here to *All Souls*, I saw a little breakfast and sandwich shop across the street on the corner. Would you go over there with me and talk some more over breakfast? It would mean so much to me, Naomi."

"Yes, John, I will go with you." I answered immediately, without hesitation because there was something in his manner and tone of voice that spoke to my heart. Inside, I felt the Lord's spirit telling me this was the right thing to do.

Walking out of the family room with John, trusting that voice inside me, I felt a strange inner peace. It was the peace that passeth all human understanding, the one only God can give us.

Getting to the elevator, we waited for it to come up from the first floor. As the doors opened, I was confronted by the last person I ever expected to see.

# CHAPTER 22

# A Way Forward

The elevator doors opened. Before our eyes, John and I found ourselves face to face with Sister Mary. She immediately started talking, "You must be John Wilson, Ruth Wilson's son. Chaplain Andrews told me you were coming."

"Yes, yes I am. And you are?"

"I'm Sister Mary. I became good friends with your mother while she was here. I gave her a picture of Jesus with the lost lamb. It seemed to comfort her."

"Thank you for your kindness. My mother was in need, and you saw that."

"John, I want to leave you with something I know. The Lord looks at people far deeper than their outward appearance. He taught me to look into one's heart to see what one really needs."

John absorbed her words, "I will remember that."

"I know you will, my son."

"Sister Mary," I broke in, "John is taking me to breakfast. I'm actually leaving these walls for a while and getting out into the world."

She looked at both of us knowingly. "The world is so confused and lost in so many ways. The future belongs to you two young people and those like you, who have faith and Christ in their hearts, to set things right. May God bless you both as you carry His royal banner out into the world beyond these walls."

John was deeply affected by her words and told her, "You're an inspiring person, Sister Mary."

"Thank you, my son, but I only say what God puts in my heart to speak."

Then I whispered words to her, straight from my heart, "You mean the world to me."

"Remember this, my child, whatever comes next for you is all part of God's miraculous hand at work in your life. It will be a way forward for you."

After that, she nodded goodbye, going to the window in the family room, where she soaked up the warmth of a new day.

John stared after her for a moment, then whispered to me, "That woman is a remarkable woman."

I answered, "You don't know how remarkable."

With that, we entered the elevator, coming out as the doors opened on the first floor. On our way to the front door, we encountered Chaplain Andrews in the lobby.

John spoke up, "Thank you for finding Miss Naomi. She's been a great help to me. I would like to talk to her some more. Would you mind if I take her to breakfast?"

"Not at all. I've been trying to get her to go outside of these walls more often."

As we exited *All Souls* into the warm light of morning, Chaplain Andrews followed us to the door, stepping outside, looking after us as we walked down the street. My guardian angel would tell me later what happened:

Chaplain Andrews was alone for a moment, but only for seconds. It was then he heard a familiar voice, "Andrews, what are you thinking?" It was the voice of Sister Mary.

Chaplain Andrews looked over toward the direction of the voice as she became visible right next to him. He answered, "I was wondering, what's happening?"

Sister Mary explained, "What's happening is that Naomi is going to help that young man become a Christian soldier."

"But what is going to happen to Naomi?"

Sister Mary already knew the answer, "She's about to begin a new chapter of her own life as a soldier for Christ. You know, Andrews, Naomi has seen the light and knows how to bring its spirit into the hearts and minds of others."

"Yes," acknowledged Chaplain Andrews, "that young woman has a gift."

Sister Mary was more definite, "It's Naomi's gift."

POSTSCRIPT: God brought John and me together. I will always believe that. Later on, we found a local church that Ann Bishop had suggested to us. Together, we found our way forward in what we were to do. Six months later, we joined a missionary group, bringing the word of the Lord to impoverished souls who did not know Him. Perhaps, one day we will return to *All Souls*. But for now, both of us feel we are doing what Christ wanted us to do.

Thinking about it, I will always cherish the memories of those months I spent at *All Souls*. In the quiet moments, I often say a silent prayer for Sister Mary, Chaplain Andrews, and all the souls I came to know and love there.

As I see awful things going on in the world around me, I remember the words of the prophet, Isaiah, that the Prince of Peace would rid the world of its chaos and bring peace to all mankind.

Doing the missionary work I do now, I've let the Lord take over, guiding me every step of the way through life. It makes me feel complete within my own heart and soul.

I'm often asked by those that come to know me, what have I learned in my life. I tell them that my life's journey has taken me, in visions, into the Light twice. Both times I encountered Jesus. He later whispered to my mind, *I am the light of the world. Whoever follows me will never walk in darkness, but will have the light of eternal life.*

I have found that God surrounds us with His love and wisdom more than anyone realizes. His presence is there if we seek it. When asked, Jesus answered, *I am with you always.*

# Author's Notes

How I came to write *Naomi's Journey Into the Light:* First of all, I had no idea that a series of unusually vivid, highly personal events would provide the initial creative spark that led me to this story. Having witnessed many deaths over the course of my life, as well as having an extremely vivid, near-death experience of my own, came together inside my mind, inspiring me to write what has become this book.

It was as though a Divine Voice from the deepest regions of my own faith was telling me this could be a book that would move and uplift the hearts of many who would read it. I kept hearing these words throughout the writing process. At the same time, I could feel the spirit of the Lord guiding me every step of the way.

This is how this story became a novel of thoughts and ideas within a character-driven narrative. Though it became the book I wanted it to be, there is so much more to be said about faith, about Jesus, the end-of-life experience, and the hope of Heaven. What can be said could fill the shelves of a vast library.

On yet another level, I wanted to show how God is involved in all our lives, just as He has been since the beginning of time. He can alter people's lives, bringing new peace and meaning to all who open up their hearts and accept His spirit into their souls. He can intervene in one's life, healing all that is broken if one lets Him. Just as the life of Naomi Larson is healed and made anew within the pages of this story, so can the life of anyone who embraces the spirit of God and becomes born again.

In completing this little volume, I have had one of the most rewarding writing experiences of my life. I feel an internal satisfaction, what I would best describe as God's peace bestowed upon me. More than ever, I believe, as Jesus said, *Through faith, all things are possible.*

In closing, may you, too, dear reader, be rewarded with a faith-inspiring experience. May the Lord enrich your life on your own journey into His light.

Sam Rawlins, January 2022

# Acknowledgements

From initial ideas, this book of faith slowly evolved into the reality of the book you hold in your hands. I want to express my deepest thanks to all who encouraged me in this process. To those who extended their kind advice and words of wisdom, you have my undying gratitude.

The longer I live, the more I have come to believe that no one has ever been truly successful without someone, a mentor perhaps, who took a special interest in the individual. In my own case, there might not have ever been 'Sam Rawlins the writer' if my life had not crossed paths with one of the greatest women of faith I have ever known. She was my grandmother who raised me, Callie Victoria Valentine. Not only did she encourage me as a young writer, but she was also one of the first to teach me the true meaning of, *through faith, all things are possible.* She raised me as her son, and on the day she died, I told her I was very proud to be her son. Even more importantly, I told her that one day I would see her in Heaven again.

Now, I wish to acknowledge a few of those individuals who have participated with me, in creative association, to transform this book from a dream into reality:

Shelly Reynolds' contributions have been a major factor here. Having been a colleague of mine on several projects over the years, she never wavered in helping to make this manuscript better through its many revisions and rewrites. Her suggestions and comments always improved the quality of the book.

To the team at Yorkshire Publishing, led by Director of Publishing, Samantha Ryan, your suggestions and advice have always been appreciated. I'm deeply grateful for the opportunity to have a third inspirational novel published under your label. I feel blessed to be with such a wonderful publisher.

Searching for the best, most inspiring cover for *Naomi's Journey Into The Light* that would embody the essence of the book led me to Doug McEntyre. With his invaluable help, a near-perfect cover has been achieved. Doug is, without question, the best Webmaster in the business.

Beyond those immediately involved, many people have quite unknowingly contributed to this book. Through their kindness and generosity to others, they have shown me the world is a much better place with them in it. Witnessing such examples never ceases to inspire me, especially in the writing of this book.

I have come to know so many amazing people in my life. For so many reasons, I thank God for allowing me to meet them. Among a few of them, there are those whom I will cherish their friendship forever.

Years from now, if I can look back, I will think of someone who had a little dog named Gracie as one of the most truly good persons I have ever known. You have given me the most valuable thing one person can give another, your friendship. I will treasure that–with all my heart–always.

It is the unselfish acts of a few good individuals that often motivates me to become a better person and a better writer. I feel so blessed to have known all the people mentioned here. My life has truly been a wonderful life because of knowing all of them.

# ALSO BY SAM RAWLINS

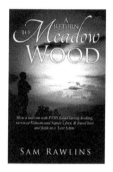
If you enjoyed **Naomi's Journey Into The Light**, you may find rewarding these two other deeply moving novels from the pen of Sam Rawlins: **A Return to Meadow Wood** is the inspiring story of a Vietnam veteran suffering from PTSD, his journey into faith, and finding lasting healing. Many readers have said this is a book that will take over your soul as you read it.

**Young Lincoln of New Salem** will get you into Lincoln's heart and soul as you read it. This is the story of Lincoln's early life in New Salem during the 1830s on the rugged Illinois frontier. This is Lincoln between the ages of 22 to 28, his life's journey into love and heartbreak, and how it would both haunt and inspire him all the rest of his life.

Both books are available in paperback, hardcover, and E-book on Amazon and Barnes and Noble.com.

CPSIA information can be obtained
at www.ICGtesting.com
Printed in the USA
BVHW072245160522
637190BV00001B/2